**Looking at ...
Dallas massaged ... her legs
and feet, still excited that she had
agreed to spend the night.**

Without the slightest hesitation, she had given him an answer to a question he'd feared asking. She had been eager to go home with him. He couldn't believe his good fortune.

Stretched out on the custom king bed in a sexy black gown, she felt red-hot and sexy.

Lanier stilled his hands. "The massage feels great, but I'm ready for the main event."

Taking in a deep breath, Dallas tried to calm his heart rate. "I love how you get straight to the point."

Lanier gave a soft, guttural growl and smiled devilishly. Taking the lotion from Dallas's hand, she set it on the nightstand. She urged him to come closer, then lay flat on her back.

Placing her hand at the nape of his neck, she guided his head until it rested between her perky breasts. "What's your pleasure, superstar?" Lanier stroked his face. "Name it."

"What about boundaries?"

Her eyes gleamed flirtatiously. "Only those you put in force."

Books by Linda Hudson-Smith

Kimani Romance

Forsaking All Others
Indiscriminate Attraction
Romancing the Runway
Destiny Calls
Kissed by a Carrington
Promises to Keep
Seduction at Whispering Lakes
Tempted by a Carrington

LINDA HUDSON-SMITH

was born in Canonsburg, Pennsylvania, and raised in Washington, Pennsylvania. After illness forced her to leave a successful marketing and public relations career, she turned to writing as a healing and creative outlet.

Linda has won several awards, including a Career Achievement Award from *RT Book Reviews*. She was also voted Best New Writer by the Black Writers Alliance, named Best New Christian Fiction Author by *Shades of Romance* magazine and Rising Star by Romance In Color. She is also a recipient of a Gold Pen award and has won two awards from the African American Literary Awards Show.

For the past decade Linda has served as a national spokesperson for the Lupus Foundation of America.

The mother of two sons, Linda lives with her husband, Rudy, in League City, Texas. To find out more go to her website, www.lindahudsonsmith.com. You can also email her at lindahudsonsmith@yahoo.com.

Tempted
by a
CARRINGTON

LINDA HUDSON-SMITH

KIMANI
ROMANCE

KIMANI PRESS™

ISBN-13: 978-0-373-86243-6

Recycling programs for this product may not exist in your area.

TEMPTED BY A CARRINGTON

www.kimanipress.com

Printed in U.S.A.

Dear Reader,

I sincerely hope you enjoy reading *Tempted by a Carrington* from cover to cover. Many of you have requested more on the hot Carrington triplets and I was only too happy to deliver another story about these popular men.

I am very interested in hearing your comments on the sizzling romance between Dallas Carrington and Lanier Watson. The couple featured has appeared in every novel written about the Carrington triplets…and they're back to settle the score between them and to recapture your hearts all over again.

Please enclose a self-addressed, stamped envelope with all of your correspondence. You can also email your comments to lindahudsonsmith@yahoo.com, and please visit my website, www.lindahudsonsmith.com.

Linda Hudson-Smith
16516 El Camino Real
Box 174
Houston, TX 77062

Chapter 1

As the mid-August sun peeked through the slightly opened slats of the white shutters in Lanier Watson's loft bedroom, she turned over on her back. Looking up at the ceiling, she closed her eyes.

Today wasn't just another ordinary day. It was the day Lanier was to meet with her parents, Barbara and Joseph, whom she hadn't seen in years. At the age of twelve, she had been placed into protective custody when her parents had gotten into a vicious physical struggle fueled by substance abuse. Lanier had entered the foster care system on that frightening night and had remained there until the age of eighteen. An academic scholarship got her into college, where she graduated at the top of her class. She'd then gotten a job as a social worker and continued her academic studies until she received a master's degree and became a medical social worker.

Lanier opened her eyes. The ability to relax and let go of her troubles felt good. With all the pain she had endured in her youth and adulthood, she hadn't found a lot to be happy about. How great she felt now indicated how committed she was to achieving a full mental recovery. It had taken her a long time to come to terms with her troubled life, but she'd done it.

A warm smile curved on Lanier's full lips. Thinking of Dallas Carrington, the tall, sexy man she loved with every ounce of her strength, always brought a smile to her face. He was one of a set of gorgeous triplets, a member of the prestigious Carrington family. Dallas, the second-born triplet, played baseball, a shortstop for the National Baseball League's Texas Hurricanes. Austin, first-born triplet, was starting quarterback for the NFL's Texas Wranglers, and Houston played power forward for the NBA's Texas Cyclones. These superstar athletes loved playing professional sports before the hometown crowds in their native Houston.

Lanier had met Dallas over three years ago on a Valentine's Day cruise. He was instantly attracted to her, but she had quickly pegged him as a man with roving eyes. As he hotly pursued her, unwilling to accept no for an answer, Lanier had eventually given in to his indelible charms. Because of her parents' volatile marriage, she had shied away from long-term commitments. Fear of abandonment was at the crux of her complex problems regarding love and romance. Dallas had been more than patient with her, but she feared his patience would run out long before she had conquered all of her insecurities.

Dallas would be at Lanier's side for the luncheon date

with her estranged parents. His presence would shore her up. Even if he hadn't been able to attend, she'd made up her mind to go through with it. Putting the reunion off for another day wasn't in anyone's best interest.

Slipping out of bed, Lanier put on her robe and made her way out into the hallway. The bounce in her step made her smile. Before heading to the winding staircase, she glanced back at the clock radio. Right on schedule, she thought. Getting her routine started at the same time every day was once very challenging. Lanier now looked forward to the comfort of the routine.

Without knocking on the adjacent bedroom door, Lanier opened it slowly and peeked inside. Not so long ago, three sleeping figures would've been lying in the empty beds.

Sisters Lauren and Stephanie Liggins were only ten months apart in age. They had occupied two of the three twin beds, which was a step up from their old bunks. Tina Rodgers would've been curled up in a ball in the third bed. The girls had just turned eighteen and would leave for college in the fall. They were now at summer camp. Their departure was hard for Lanier, but there was currently a long waiting list for foster placement at Haven House.

Although the owners of Haven House preferred teenagers, they'd accept most school-age females. No males had resided at Haven House thus far. Former foster children themselves, Lanier and her best friend, Ashleigh Ayers-Carrington, thought they could best serve teenage females.

It didn't matter that the young women had to move

on. The two female social workers would always be there for the girls. They loved the young women as if they were their own sisters. After Ashleigh had married and become pregnant, Lanier's duties had doubled. It had taken her a long time to hire help when Ashleigh started working part-time. It had taken even longer for Lanier to fully trust the new employees.

"Rise and shine," Lanier would've sung out cheerfully, followed by an enthusiastic, "You all know the drill." The teenagers would pop out of bed and drowsily greet Lanier. Once they had begun their morning rituals, Lanier would go back upstairs and shower and dress for the day. There was always plenty to do around Haven House. With two other employees to help out, the daily grind had finally become a lot easier for everyone to bear.

Dressed in a chic white linen pantsuit and gold silk top and white pumps, Lanier looked fabulous. Her mahogany skin glowed. Not one for too much makeup, she had only dusted her face with loose powder to combat any shine. She loved lipstick and glosses. The rich Bordeaux shade she wore was a perfect match for her skin tone.

As Lanier entered the empty kitchen, a lump formed in her throat, making it difficult for her to swallow. It was getting harder for her to hide her emotions as of late. All she could think about was the girls who would soon leave for college. There was an endless list of others who needed foster placement, but these young girls had been the first to reside at Haven House. That alone made them very special to Lanier and Ashleigh.

* * *

Lanier licked her lips in anticipation of Dallas's sweet kiss. Tall, with a toffee-brown complexion and too sexy to be legal, he made her pulse quicken just by stepping into her line of vision. His ebony eyes encompassed her in a way that calmed her fears. Ever since she'd first met the hottest shortstop for the National Baseball League's Texas Hurricanes, he'd had a drugging effect on her senses. Although Dallas had had roving eyes on the Valentine's Day cruise where she'd first met him, she still had ended up falling hard.

Their relationship had developed quickly, and they had lots of fun getting to know one another. After a few months of exclusive dating, Dallas began to make sexual moves on Lanier. The all-of-a-sudden fast pace in which he'd come at her had Lanier repeatedly slowing down his intimate advances. When heated moments escalated to heights she was uncomfortable with, she had to put on the brakes to remain in control.

Although Dallas had grown sexually frustrated, none of her attempts to keep him at arm's length had chased him away. He eventually made Lanier see that he was an exceptionally good guy and that she should hold on to him. Nothing about her past or her family's issues had put him off. He had remained beyond supportive.

Lowering her lashes, Lanier moved into Dallas's warm embrace. Tilting her head back, she gave him easy access to her lips, which were hungry for the sweet taste of his. His mouth pressed down over hers, making her body melt like hot candle wax. As his tongue coiled around hers, her insides fluttered.

Holding Lanier slightly away from him, Dallas

looked down into her eyes. "No matter what happens today, don't forget I'll be there for you. No one will ever hurt you again."

Lanier's heart skipped a beat. "How can I ever forget it? And I'll be just fine, Dallas. I'm fully prepared to handle this meeting."

The surprised look in Dallas's eyes was easy enough for her to read—he hadn't expected her to be so confident.

If only he knew...and he would definitely come to know if she had her way.

If Lanier Watson had her way, Dallas was in for a super treat. As he got acquainted with the new and improved her, she hoped the bad memories of how she once was would fade from his memory bank. Before the first time they'd made love, she'd lost count of the times she had put him off or had attempted to break up with him. Always spoiling for a fight, her angry attitude and sullen ways would've had the average guy dropping her like a hot potato.

Lanier's memory of her countless horrendously bad moods hurt her the most because they'd injured Dallas emotionally. Still, he'd stayed by her side, blaming her past for her presiding issues. Their rockiest times had actually made her a better person. Dallas had been her catalyst for change. Her love for him had her wanting their relationship to work, but she had to make some more adjustments in her flippant attitude and negative mind-set.

Getting help from a therapist hadn't gone well, but Lanier had gained enough courage to try to move past old devastations. Dallas didn't know the Lanier she wanted to be, and she couldn't wait to introduce him to the brand-new lady in his life. She had all sorts of grandiose ideas to show off her new self to him. Nothing was as important as proving to him that she was ready to receive his love, all of it. No more ducking, dodging and running. Lanier had been enchantingly tempted by a Carrington triplet—and now she was ready to be captured.

The elder Watsons hadn't yet arrived at the Golden Dragon, one of Dallas's favorite Chinese restaurants. The bold reds, bright gold and ebony and alabaster hues were perfect tones for an authentic Asian space.

Glancing at her watch, Lanier had mixed emotions about her parents' tardiness. Instead of making a big deal out of it, like the old her would've done, she tried to be grateful for the extra time to make sure she had herself pulled together. The hostess had already seated them at a spacious yet private table.

"Do you want a drink while we wait?" Dallas asked.

Lanier smiled. "A cup of hot tea would be nice."

Leaning toward Lanier, Dallas kissed her cheek. "You got it." He summoned the waiter.

Before the server could return with the order, a hostess ushered Barbara and Joseph to where Lanier and Dallas awaited their arrival.

Dallas glanced at Lanier, his expression quickly turning to one of concern. She had gotten to her feet before he'd been able to take her hand and squeeze it for reassurance. She had harbored so much bitterness for her parents that he wondered if she were truly ready to see them.

"Mom, Dad," Lanier said sweetly, swallowing the foreign words that had once tasted like battery acid. But now she didn't feel the least bit bitter calling Barbara and Joseph "Mom and Dad." "It's nice to see you. Please have a seat."

Lanier immediately introduced her parents to Dallas without revealing his profession. As far as she could remember, her father had never taken an interest in sports.

Joseph's face was blank as he shook Dallas's hand. Barbara looked nervous. The older woman was the same height as her daughter, and the father was several inches taller. Lanier had inherited her mother's creamy mahogany complexion, but Dallas thought she looked more like her father. She had his eyes, nose and satiny hair texture.

Dallas relaxed in his seat. "It's nice to finally meet you, Mr. and Mrs. Watson. You have a lovely daughter."

"Thank you," the couple said simultaneously, both appearing fidgety.

Barbara made direct eye contact with Lanier. "I'm glad you finally agreed to see us. Have you received my letters?"

Lanier nodded. "I read every one. I'm glad you guys found your way back to each other. Life hasn't been easy for any of us, and I laid the blame at your feet. Building a meaningful relationship won't happen overnight, but this is a great start. Thanks for accepting my invitation to lunch. We have a lot to catch up on."

Lanier's last statement was another bombshell for Dallas since he'd assumed her parents had requested the luncheon. She had certainly done a complete about-face. As relieved as it made him feel, he still couldn't help being concerned for her. She had attempted to pull it all together a couple of times before, only to fall apart again.

Once the orders had been taken, Barbara turned and looked squarely at Lanier.

"I know you don't want us to visit the past, Lanier," Barbara said, "but I think we'll have to at some point. How can we possibly move forward without discussing it?"

Dallas tensed. Reaching for Lanier's hand, he squeezed it reassuringly.

Lanier shook her head. "We can't go back there. If we did, we can't change a thing. I like living in the present," she said adamantly.

Dallas was in awe of how strongly Lanier had voiced her desire to leave the past behind. It was a big change for a thirty-year-old woman who had constantly wallowed in the excruciating pain of the past, reliving all of life's horrors from before and after Child Protective Services had removed her from her home.

The food arrived.

"Please bow your heads," Joseph requested softly.

Lanier angled an eyebrow. She listened intently as Joseph began to pray. She heard strong conviction in his voice, and it was mind-blowing. In a recent letter to Lanier, Barbara had said she and Joseph had gotten baptized at a church they'd joined. She had found the news hard to believe, but hearing her dad praying so sincerely nearly had her convinced.

The meal was eaten and surprisingly easy conversations took place between bites. Lanier purposely steered clear of her life in foster homes, but she was proud to talk about her experience with the girls residing at Haven House. Much to Lanier's surprise, she was comfortable talking to her parents.

Less than an hour later everyone had finished their meals.

Taking the napkin from her lap, Lanier placed it on the table. "Are you still living in Clear Lake? If I recall correctly, it was in the return address."

Barbara gave a hint of a smile. "We recently moved to Dickinson."

Lanier felt a small surge of anxiety overtaking her. Dickinson was a few miles from Haven House. Trying to regroup and calm herself, she covertly drew in deep breaths.

"Dickinson is a nice place," Dallas said, hoping to give Lanier time to recover. "Most areas in southeast Houston are great places to live."

"We like it there," Joseph remarked. "It's not far from where we used to live."

Yeah, from where the state was forced to remove me from the home I once loved, Lanier thought, *only to send me to places that were worse.*

Joseph had begun drinking early on in the marriage, but it was a few years before Barbara had joined him. Hating the negative thoughts invading her mind, Lanier quickly shut them down, reminding herself she'd moved on and had made a brand-new home for herself.

Lanier made a pretense of looking at her watch. It didn't matter how much time had or hadn't elapsed, she was ready to go. "I hope everyone enjoyed their meal. I know I did. Maybe we can do this another time, but I need to get back to Haven House." She stood quickly.

* * *

Taking Lanier's keys from her hand, Dallas opened the front door to Haven House. Slinging his arm around her shoulder, he led her into the residence and headed to the family room. They both felt lethargic and were ready to relax, but he would get his cues from Lanier.

The family room was the girls' favorite hangout, and its emptiness caused Lanier's heart to ache. She knew it was silly of her, but it didn't ease the gut-wrenching pain she felt deep down inside. Making her way over to the leather sectional, she dropped down onto a reclining end.

Lanier peered up at Dallas. "Can you stay for a while? I'd like to talk to you."

Dallas shrugged. "Not a problem."

He scooted next to her and she took his hand into hers. Lifting it, she kissed each of his fingertips. "Thanks for today and every other day we've spent together. How do you think I did at lunch?"

Dallas tilted his head to the side. "How do you think you did?"

Lanier pulled a comical face. "I handled all of it very well. It was strange seeing my parents after all this time, but I wasn't bitter or uncomfortable."

"I thought you did great. I was surprised a time or two because of things I had assumed."

Lanier raised an eyebrow. "Like what?"

"I assumed they had extended the invitation to lunch. You came across as very confident, but I expected you to be nervous and antsy. When we've talked about your parents in your past, you always ended up crying your heart out."

"It still hurts, but I've found constructive ways to try and deal with it. Not thinking about it all the time helps the wounds heal. I'm much happier, Dallas, and I am more confident."

Lanier talked about all the things she'd done wrong in their relationship and how it had related to the pain of her past. "I couldn't pull myself out of the fire back then. I took everything out on you, causing so many problems in our relationship. Unwittingly, I tried to run you out of my life. I expected you to also abandon me."

"I'm glad you know the truth. I stayed because I love you, Lanier. I saw past your pain."

Fighting off her tears, her gaze dropped down to the floor then back to him. "Do you ever think of getting a new girlfriend?" She grimaced. The words hadn't come out right.

Dallas looked puzzled. "I'm perfectly happy with the one I have."

Lanier grinned. "That's nice to know. Still, I'd like to introduce you to a woman who is reinventing herself. You deserve the best."

Dallas frowned. "Did someone slip something into your drink at the restaurant? You're talking crazy. What's happened to you?"

"You happened to me, Dallas Carrington." Capturing his lips with hers, Lanier kissed him passionately. She then laid her head upon his chest. "Thanks for letting me know you're happy with me. I couldn't be any happier than I am when I'm with you. I'm the new woman I'd like you to meet. I've done so much work to try and improve me."

Lanier hoped she wasn't coming off as a lunatic.

Making a show of wiping his brow, Dallas smiled. "Now you're talking my language. You had me worried there for a minute. I just happen to love the woman you are. Any improvements might be too much for this man."

Lanier pursed her lips. "Hmm, I never thought of it like that." She grinned. "But I think you'll be very interested in meeting this person. The new and improved me, transforming by my own design."

Wrapping her arms around Dallas's neck, she kissed him deeply.

Dallas wiggled his brows. "A new you, huh? I guess I can agree to meet her, but only if you promise to send her away immediately if I don't like her."

"I promise." Lanier gave Dallas her brightest smile.

He ran his thumb over her lower lip. "Are these the things you wanted to talk about?"

"It's part of it." Lanier wrung her hands together. "Lately, I've done a lot of thinking about my future. It feels so strange around here without the girls. I miss them."

"They've grown up, Lanier, but they won't forget you. Those girls are yours and Ashleigh's for life. You two have created an unbreakable bond with the beautiful young ladies you helped raise."

She wrinkled her nose. "I know. You know how I tend to second-guess myself. It just seems like I'll be throwing them out in the street come fall. I've been where they once were and also where they're going. I don't want them to ever feel abandoned."

Dallas pulled Lanier closer to him. "That won't happen. They know what love is because of you and

Ashleigh. You won't lose a single one. Going off to college will be good for everyone."

Lanier managed a half smile. "I hope you're right." She paused for a moment. "There's something else I've also thought a lot about." Her eyes narrowed slightly. "I've never lived alone. In every foster home I've lived in, there has always been at least five or six other kids."

"I hadn't thought of that. Once my brothers and I went off to college, we only came home for holidays and school breaks, no matter how much we missed our parents. After college, we bought our own homes."

"How *did* Ms. Angelica cope with all of you leaving home at once?"

"Oh, she missed us a lot, but Dad constantly reminded her that we were no longer little boys. They'd raised us to become men. Setting children free is a normal part of life. Just remember that the girls might not have gotten an opportunity to go to college if they'd been placed elsewhere. Not all foster homes are like the one you and Ashleigh have created."

"I know that, and it'll eventually be okay. Once the girls are off to college, I think I should get my own place. Working and living here with the kids is all I've known since I resigned my social work position. I want to experience life on my own. I'm thinking of asking two of our assistants to move in here before any new kids arrive. I'll still work here ten to twelve hours a day, but I want to be able to escape sometimes."

Dallas sat up straight. "You're serious about this, aren't you? I didn't know you wanted to live anywhere but here."

"I didn't either, not until recently. But I want to reinvent myself, so I need to make substantial changes in my life. I've never lived alone. Before I moved in with Ashleigh, I had college roommates. After graduation, I shared an apartment with two other women. Ashleigh lives at home and works here…and she's satisfied with how well it works out. I'm excited about looking for a place of my own."

Dallas liked the plan, but he couldn't help wondering what this might mean for their relationship. He wasn't sure if she was ready for a major move, but the one thing he didn't want to do was put shackles on her dreams. She *was* a grown woman who obviously needed to be free.

"Would you consider living with me?" He knew he had said the wrong thing as soon as the words had left his mouth. He realized she needed to do this on her own and should've offered his support.

Massaging Dallas's cheek with the back of her hand, Lanier's heart raced. "I know why you asked that question. But please believe in me. I know what I want to do, and I know exactly why I feel that way."

Closing his hand over Lanier's, Dallas halted her nervous tapping. "I'm sure you do. And I *do* regret it—it wasn't a supportive remark. You're a big girl now and you can take care of yourself. If you can't, I'm positive you'll ask for help. Speaking of help, do you want me to help you find a place? I know the condo Houston bought a while back is empty and he doesn't stay there nearly as much as he'd thought. Maybe he'd lease it."

"Thanks, but I don't want to lease from your brother. I'd like to live close to Haven House, not in downtown Houston. I'd love for you to house-shop with me."

Dallas looked pleased. "Just tell me when you want to get started."

"This weekend? When can you manage to get away for a few hours?"

"This is the playoffs, and game dates are set as teams advance. I'll look into it. Hopefully, we can get you your own place before the finals."

Ashleigh popped into the room just as Dallas and Lanier sealed their deal with a kiss. She normally called Lanier first, but her cell phone battery had died.

Lanier sprang up and took baby Austin from Ashleigh's arms. "Hey, little A.C. Heard you've been hanging with the ladies today! I know grandma had a ball with you." She kissed the center of his forehead. "Where'd you guys go?" Lanier asked Ashleigh.

"Baybrook Mall. I just dropped by here to collect figures for payroll. I plan to print checks at home again. Is that okay?"

"However you do it is fine with me. Dallas and I just finished making plans for him to help me look for a place."

"Austin and I can also help out if you want. I can't believe preseason is almost here. Austin has enjoyed the baby so much that I think he may have a hard time getting his mind back on football."

"I know he will," Dallas chimed in. "He's having the time of his life with A.C. All he talks about is his wife and son. I get a real kick out of hearing him gushing over you two."

Dallas came over and stood next to Lanier. As he reached out for the cooing baby, she carefully handed him over to his big, strapping uncle.

Watching Dallas intently, Lanier saw how sweet and tender he was toward his nephew. He rained kisses onto the baby's shock of copper curls and A.C. cooed even more. His hair was just like Ashleigh's, but the deep dimple in his chin was a Carrington trait.

Lanier couldn't help wondering what a baby from Dallas would look like. She hadn't always wanted to become a mother, but after mothering teenagers, she had thought about it.

Since alcoholism was hereditary, Lanier wondered if the awful addiction would plague her own children. She had always been able to control her personal intake of alcohol; an occasional glass of wine or a frozen margarita was all she drank.

Seeing how engrossed Dallas and Lanier were with her son, Ashleigh cleared her throat to grab their attention. "It's time for me to get on home. There are at least a couple loads of laundry waiting for me, and Austin requested a beef rib roast for dinner."

Lanier sucked her teeth. "I don't understand why you don't use Ms. Stella more. Austin pays her no matter what."

"I love taking care of my family, so I just save Ms. Stella for special occasions. Austin really appreciates whatever I do around the house, but he's always telling me to use our housekeeper more."

If they were to ever marry, Dallas wondered if Lanier would rather have a housekeeper than take care of things herself. Either way was fine with him. His father, Beaumont, had more than enough money to pay for help, but Angelica had done everything. She had used caterers only on special occasions.

Beaumont had always helped out with kitchen duties and laundry, and Dallas could remember him and his brothers laughing at the variety of aprons their dad so proudly wore. He wasn't afraid of tackling any domestic chore and loved working alongside his beautiful wife.

Ashleigh reached for her child. Baby Austin grinned broadly, stretching his arms out for her. "I'll see you two soon. Carrington family dinner is next week, and I'm counting on you both to be there."

Dallas and Lanier nodded, laughing at Ashleigh's attempt at sternness. Walking over to his sister-in-law, he laid his hand loosely about her waist. "I'll come outside and help you get A.C. settled in." Dallas turned to Lanier. "I'll be right back, sweetheart."

After opening the rear door to the Mercedes SUV, Dallas tucked Austin into his car seat and secured the safety belt. As the baby cooed and blew spit bubbles, he had to laugh. He hadn't given much thought to having children before his nephew had come along, but now he thought about it too often.

Lanier was the only woman Dallas had ever imagined as the mother of his babies. Not wanting to pressure her, he'd never asked her if she wanted children. But, before any of that, he'd first have to find a way to get her down the aisle.

Crossing his arms, Dallas leaned against the door of the SUV. "What do you *really* think of Lanier getting her own place?"

Looking thoughtful, Ashleigh pressed together her full lips. "I support her one hundred percent. She lived in foster homes with other children and always had a roommate as an adult. Experiencing life on her own terms may be just what she needs. What's your take on it?"

Dallas raised an eyebrow. "Mixed emotions, I'm afraid. I want to support her, but I also wonder if she's ready to live alone. She's certainly changing. In fact, she promises to introduce me to the new her."

Ashleigh laughed. "That sounds just like my girl. She *does* have a creative side. I suggest you go along with her plans. What'll you do if her mission fails?"

Dallas shrugged, thinking of the angry Lanier who seemed hell-bent on self-destruction. Having faith in no one but Ashleigh had made it hard for him to earn her trust. Her unhappiness loomed over her like a terminal illness. She didn't have faith in him in the beginning, but his actions and unyielding support proved him worthy of her trust.

"Love her as much as I do now. More than anything, I want her to love herself, unconditionally. I don't want her to make any changes for me. It's all about her."

"It *is* about her. But if she falls again, be ready to catch her. She's confessed to changing her negative way of thinking about life before. She was sure she could rid herself of the rage she felt inside. We both know how badly those episodes turned out when she couldn't stay the course. Lanier may truly be ready to embrace a more positive attitude this time around. I've seen quite a few changes in her already."

Dallas stroked his chin. "Like what?" Dallas had seen major changes in Lanier, but he wanted to hear about the differences in her that Ashleigh had observed.

"You'll have to see for yourself, if you haven't already. You will recognize them on your own. It'll mean more to you and her." Standing on tiptoes, Ashleigh kissed Dallas's cheek. "See you soon, shortstop," she said. "Are you aware that Houston is hosting our family dinner?"

Dallas laughed. "So I've heard. He'll either get Mom and Kelly to cook the food or leave it up to his caterer."

Ashleigh climbed up into the SUV, leaving the door open. "Don't be too sure about that. Kelly cooks for Houston, but she also has him help. I won't be surprised if they manage to get everything taken care of between them. Ever since your brother and Kelly got engaged, he's become a changed man."

"As hard as it is to believe, I think you're right." Dallas turned down his mouth at the corners. "I guess we'll wait and see what happens with Houston and Dr. Kelly Charleston. Drive carefully, Ash. Tell Austin I'll call him later. You guys are coming to my next home game, aren't you?"

"Of course we are. We already got a babysitter."

Dallas blew Ashleigh a kiss. "See you soon." He waited until Ashleigh had backed the vehicle out of the driveway before returning to the house.

Dallas reclaimed his seat on the sofa. While waiting for Lanier to return from the kitchen, he gave more thought to her plan. If he had his way, she'd live in a gated community with security guards. But he had to be careful not to dictate his wants to her.

Carrying a plastic tray laden with two glasses of ice-cold raspberry lemonade and warmed-up takeout food, Lanier slowly walked back into the family room. She set the tray down on the coffee table and handed a glass to Dallas. "I hope you like this new recipe."

Taking the glass, he smiled. "Thanks. It looks delicious. I know I'll like it simply because you made it." He took one long gulp.

Lanier chuckled at how he'd nearly drained the glass in one swallow. He *was* a big man, and it still amazed her that he could down an entire quart of milk during breakfast or over a late-night snack of cookies.

"Are you familiar with the brand-new town houses on Clear Lake City Boulevard?"

"I've seen them a time or two," Dallas said. "Want to check them out?"

She nodded. "I'll call first to check out the cost. I don't want to get there and end up embarrassed if I can't afford it."

Dallas began eating, polishing his food off quickly. "It's time for me to go." He got to his feet. "I've got a few things to take care of. Walk me to the door?"

Lanier stood, playfully bumping his body with hers. "What are you doing later?"

"I haven't made any plans. Want to hang out with me? I can bring a couple movies."

Lanier smiled. "I'd like that. Why don't you just come back for dinner? Hamburgers and French fries are on the menu. Sound good to you?"

"Just being with you sounds good to me. Want me to stop somewhere and pick up burgers, fries and shakes?"

Leaning into Dallas, Lanier kissed him softly on the mouth. "You just show up. I'll take care of the rest."

Taking Lanier into his arms, Dallas kissed her thoroughly, loving how soft and pliable her juicy lips were. He loved it when things were going right with the woman he loved.

Chapter 2

Deciding at the last minute to take a detour, Dallas exited I-45 South onto Clear Lake City Boulevard. A few minutes down the road, he pulled up to the gates of the City on the Lake townhomes, which Lanier had mentioned. After telling the guard he was there to view model homes, the gate was opened. He hoped Lanier wouldn't think he was prying into her private affairs by finding out information on the complex.

Opening the door, Dallas stepped into the air-conditioned office.

Smiling all over the place, the lady behind the front desk rushed to her feet. "Hello!" She extended her hand to Dallas. "I'm Casey Rayburn. Are you interested in our complex?"

"I'm not looking to move, but I have a friend who is. I'd like to see the models."

Casey suddenly turned pale. "Oh, my goodness,

you're one of the Carrington triplets. I'm not sure which one, but I follow you in sports. I won't try to guess which brother you are."

Smiling broadly, she hunched her shoulders. "Can you just tell me? I'm dying to know."

Smiling back at her, Dallas removed his hand from her tight grip. "I'm Dallas, member of the Texas Hurricanes. Thanks for supporting us. We appreciate it."

"I can't think of anyone in Texas who doesn't support you. Ladies go crazy when any one of you guys is on television. I didn't know much about sports until you all started playing." She suddenly looked embarrassed. "Sorry for kind of losing it. I'm sure you didn't come in here to see me act a fool. How many bedrooms is your friend interested in?"

Dallas stroked his chin. "Don't know for sure. I'll take a guess that she'd want two or maybe three. I'll just look at all four models. Are they open?"

"Yes." Grabbing a folder off the counter, she handed it to him. "Inside are copies of the floor plans for each town house, including square footage and pricing sheets. The end units cost more. Every unit has an attached two-car garage. Let me know if you have any questions."

"Thanks." Dallas exited out of French doors that led to the models.

The first town house Dallas entered had three bedrooms and three full baths. The flooring throughout the house was laid with both hardwood and ceramic tile. The roomy end unit had over 2,500 square feet of living space, including a fabulous sunroom with a great lake view. The master suite was located downstairs. Racing upstairs, he immediately liked the warm feel of the entire unit, and he was sure Lanier would give it a thumbs-up.

Imagining Lanier in these lavish surroundings was easy for Dallas. Three years of being together had given him insight into her likes and dislikes. She loved soft and silky things next to her body, and she loved European furnishings. Visions of her moving around in the town house made him smile. He still had more models to view, but his heart had embraced this one.

Moving toward the next townhome, Dallas opened the front door and walked in. The warmth he'd felt in the first residence was noticeably absent. The place was beautifully furnished and well-appointed, but something was missing. This townhome had two bedrooms and two full baths. Moving upstairs, he hurried through each room. It had been much easier for him to savor the splendor in the first home. Simply put, this house was by no means a perfect fit for Lanier. It was nice enough, but nowhere near up to her standard.

The next two models weren't as well-appointed as the first town house, Dallas noted. If Lanier could fit the first one into her budget, he was willing to bet she'd go for it. All she'd have to do was put her stamp of approval on it and pen her signature. He'd also read that one of the subdivisions inside the complex had town houses for purchase. Purchasing may be a much better option for Lanier than leasing, but he wasn't certain of her interest.

Dallas pulled his Mercedes into the driveway at Haven House. He'd fallen asleep after a hot shower and was glad he'd made it back on time for dinner.

Lanier reached Dallas before he made it out of the car. The bright smile on her face had his heart thumping wildly. "Hey, there, beautiful," he said, taking her into his arms. Lanier had never come outside to meet him like this. Dallas took it to mean she was in a good mood and was happy to see him.

Dallas had already eaten two double-decker burgers and a large salad before he decided to mind his manners. Lanier had been closely watching him from the first bite he'd taken. Her spurts of giggles weren't lost on him. She was still as fascinated as most people were by the amount of food he consumed.

"Who are the Hurricanes playing day after tomorrow?" Lanier asked.

"Toronto Mustangs. They're a good team, but we're better. Hopefully, we'll get the win." He smiled. "Did you get your ticket from Ashleigh?"

"Got it yesterday," Lanier replied. She stood. "Okay, Dallas, its dish-duty time."

Dallas jumped up from his seat. "Let's get it done. Then we can cuddle on the couch and watch a movie or two."

Lanier loved lazy nights in with him. Her eyes filled with pride every time she thought about how he'd hotly pursued her on the cruise ship. It had taken her a while to respond to his flirtations because she had tagged him a playboy on sight, but she was wrong. She winked at him. "You're the best."

The couple vacated the clean kitchen and went into the family room, where they curled up together on the sofa. Outside of hugs and light kisses, there'd never been any heavy intimacy between them inside Haven House. Lanier was a positive role model for the girls, and she wouldn't do anything to jeopardize that.

After pulling Lanier's legs across his lap, Dallas handed her a large brown envelope. "I checked out those town houses we talked about earlier. The information is inside."

Lanier smiled. Before she would have balked at Dallas taking matters into his own hands, but the new Lanier was downright grateful. She was over being suspicious of the intent of others.

Up until Lanier had met Ashleigh, she had trusted no one. Her best friend and confidante had shown her time and time again how trustworthy she was. Their loyal friendship and respect for each other had allowed them to become and remain successful business partners.

Putting her arms around Dallas, Lanier clasped her hands together at his nape. "Have I told you lately how amazing you are?"

"You can tell me again. It's music to my ears." Giving in to his desire to kiss her breath away, he pressed his lips against hers, sweetly devouring them.

Lanier took a minute to glance over the information in the packet. "I'd still like you to look at the town houses with me. Is that okay?"

"Sure. I can take you on Sunday. I don't have to report to the field house until late afternoon."

"Hope I get an idea of what I want when I go take a look."

"If I get here Sunday morning, at 9:45 or so, is that good for you?"

"It's fine." Looking into his eyes, she ran the back of

her hand down the side of his face. "I want desperately to give back what you give me. This time around I'm going to make us work. I promise. I love you, Dallas."

Wrapping her up in his arms, he seared her lips with another hot, moist kiss. "I can't get enough of you. I love you, too. And I always root for us."

Lanier smiled broadly. "As long as we're honest and up front with each other, we can make it work."

Dallas knew he could live up to whatever expectations Lanier had of him. The only question in his mind was if he she was ready to be open to the relationship. Her skittish behaviors of the past still concerned him. At one time, fear was all she'd known. He'd love it if she could accept him at face value and love him for the genuine, honest man he was.

Dallas got up from the sofa then reached a hand back to Lanier. As she arose and stood with him, he kissed her tenderly on the mouth. He'd been dying to ask how many kids she wanted to have one day, but the fear of scaring her had kept him mute on the subject. Lanier had never mentioned wanting kids, but he knew she'd make a good mother just by the way she interacted with the girls. Besides that, he didn't know if she'd ever agree to marry him, or anyone else.

Dallas only planned to propose once more. If Lanier turned him down again, he had silently promised himself to end the romance. After nearly two years of exclusive dating, he had popped the question during a family vacation cruise to celebrate Angelica's birthday. Lanier had been deeply moved by the sentiment, but she was clearly not ready to make a lifetime commitment to him. Her tearful reply had confirmed the bad news. Yet he was sure she loved him—and he loved her enough to wait.

Dallas turned his full attention on Lanier, who had bent over to insert a CD. Her perfectly rounded rear excited him. Everything about her was electrifying. Most of all, he loved her tenacity. Just when it looked as if she might give up on something, she'd dig her heels in hard. Her life hadn't been the least bit easy, but she'd done far more than just survive.

If their love affair could endure Lanier's insecurities, which were largely based on her issues of abandonment and her parents' alcohol and drug use, their problems would be solved. The worry of being abandoned again kept her on edge. One minute she was fearful of being left behind and scared of becoming an alcoholic. Because of her anxieties, she was unwilling to commit. Scared stiff of being rejected and tossed aside, especially by the man she loved so deeply, she kept a protective shield around her fragile heart. Dallas knew they could live happily ever after, but Lanier had to believe it, too. He was still willing to bet high stakes on them.

Lanier came over to Dallas and extended her hand to him. "Want to get in a little bumping and grinding on the dance floor?" Her eyelashes batted flirtatiously.

Not about to turn down such an enthralling offer, Dallas grinned. "How far and how low can we go?"

"Tsk, tsk," Lanier scolded. "You know the answer. We've never done anything over the top here. The girls may be gone, but their presence isn't."

Dallas swept her into his arms. Pulling her as close to his body as he could, he hungrily engaged his mouth with hers. Bumping and grinding their hips together was sensuous. He wondered who'd be the first one to put on the brakes. His willpower was definitely in doubt.

Laying her head on Dallas's chest, Lanier closed her eyes, inhaling his manly scent. With her arms wound loosely around Dallas's neck, the couple's body rhythms matched perfectly the sexy, provocative music. If she were anywhere other than Haven House, she'd be tempted to strip and dance provocatively for his pleasure. It wasn't something she'd done before, but he made her feel uninhibited. The thought of stripping for him had her hot. Lanier could barely wait to make it happen.

As a much faster paced song came on, Lanier and Dallas let the music take them over. As she ground her hips into his, he pulled her back against him. His manhood rose as he matched her wild, sexy moves. For the next several minutes, they stay locked together, bumping and grinding to the music.

They headed back to the sofa and sat down to catch their breath. She picked up the remote control. "Where are the movies?"

Dallas snapped his fingers. "Out in the car. I'll get them."

"Let's look at the cable guide first. We can surf the movie channels and maybe there'll be something on. I don't want you out of my sight." She blew him a kiss.

Dallas didn't care if the screen was blank. Lanier was always doing or saying something that turned him on, without even realizing it. When she'd bent over the CD player earlier, it had taken all his strength to keep from taking her down to the carpet and making wild, passionate love to her. Dallas would never disrespect the sacredness of Haven House, but he had no control over the X-rated thoughts that ran through his mind.

Stopping on a cable channel, Lanier watched what was happening on the screen for several seconds before she realized it was an erotic flick. She stole a glance at Dallas, but he appeared unaffected by what was on television. Instead of turning the channel, she set down the remote. Without uttering a word, she got comfortable, laying her head on Dallas's lap.

Inwardly, she laughed, knowing he was wondering what had gotten into her. If he had turned on an erotic movie, he'd expect her to throw a fit. The old Lanier might've been offended, but she was trying to lighten up.

His eyes darting between Lanier and the television screen, Dallas couldn't help wondering if she was really comfortable with the heavy eroticism. He didn't normally watch these types of shows, but her enjoying it made him feel sexy.

It didn't take Dallas long to get worked up. He reached for Lanier and kissed her passionately. His hand snaked up under her top and fondled each of her breasts, and his breathing was labored. Just as he was about to unsnap her bra straps, she jumped up, making him feel bad for attempting to heat up her body.

Lanier's eyes appeared apologetic. "I'm sorry. I can't do this here."

He stood. "It's okay. I was out of line, and I'm sorry." He took a deep breath. "I'm leaving now. I want to make love to you…and I can't."

Lanier felt awful, but she couldn't bring herself to engage in lovemaking at Haven House.

This was her fault, she knew. It started with the offer of bumping and grinding while dancing. She had been sexually affected by what was on the television screen, so she should've expected Dallas to feel something, too. The erotic movie had made her just as hot as he was.

He touched his lips lightly to her forehead. "Good night. See you tomorrow."

Lanier hated to see their evening end like so many of their past dates. He was sexually frustrated, and she was to blame. She had to change her position about Haven House. It was the girls' home, but it was also hers. The girls weren't here, and Dallas had been so close. Now she felt sad and lonely. It had been hard to see him go, and she should've asked him to stay.

In white jeans and a sexy orange sleeveless top, Lanier stepped outside the house to wait for Dallas. She sat on the porch swing and laid her purse beside her. As she looked around at the beautiful flowers and shrubs, she smiled, remembering when Haven House looked like it should've been condemned. Instead it had been sold to her and Ashleigh way below market value. A lot of hard work and money had gone into restoring the home to a beautiful property.

Dallas's silver Mercedes-Benz came into view. By the time she reached the vehicle, he was out of the car, making his way around to the passenger side.

He gently kissed her forehead. "Sweetheart, you look gorgeous."

Dallas brought Lanier into his arms and kissed her passionately. His manhood readily responded to the mere feel of her, but now was not the time for his virility to react so wildly to her sexiness. Last night's disappointing episode was enough for him. Holding Lanier slightly away from him, his ebony eyes connected with hers. "Is everything okay?"

Lanier nodded. "It couldn't be better. I can't wait to tour the town houses."

Ten minutes later Dallas drove his car through security gates and parked. Leaning across the seat, he kissed Lanier. "Sit tight. I'll open your door."

Extending his hand to Lanier, Dallas helped her exit. Physical contact with her sent another jolt of electricity right through him. All he could do was wish they were off somewhere alone so he could make love to her endlessly.

Hand in hand, Dallas and Lanier walked through the neighborhood, her eyes drinking in the lush landscaping. She already liked the feel of this place. The atmosphere was peaceful. Living alone still scared her, but she couldn't move forward in her life without having the experience.

Opening the office door, Dallas allowed Lanier to precede him.

"Let's start with the last model and work our way back to the first," he suggested.

"Good idea. Model home sites tend to save the best for last."

They entered the model and looked around. Dallas checked for signs of approval or disapproval on Lanier's face. She was expressionless, making it impossible for him to read her.

"It doesn't feel warm to me. It's nice but lacks something I can't put my finger on. Trying to imagine it without furnishings is hard. I wish models were empty so visitors could see it frill-free," she remarked.

The couple went upstairs, but Lanier still looked unimpressed.

Dallas pursed his lips. "Ready to move on to the next one?"

"May as well. This one is not for me."

Dallas took Lanier's hand and led her back downstairs. As they reached the exit, he pulled her to him suddenly and united their lips in a tender kiss. As his sex responded to the feel of her body close to his, his mouth increased the pressure on hers.

Dallas ended the kiss, but Lanier took up where he'd left off. Her hunger for him had her crazy with desire as she rubbed against his thickened organ pressing against her thigh. Even though she was in public, she had no problem envisioning them making love.

Raw passion in her eyes made Dallas gulp hard. "In a naughty-girl mood, huh?"

"You can say that. If I wasn't worried about someone walking in on us, I'd tempt you to take me right here."

Feeling the intense heat of her body, Dallas felt as if he were sweating from within. It was selfish of him, but he'd been fantasizing about her moving away from Haven House. Their lovemaking was restricted because of her position as foster mother. Even when she spent a night at his home, she couldn't relax completely because she had to remain in control of herself.

Letting go and completely freeing inhibitions was difficult for someone filled with fear. He loved spending time with her at Haven House, but so many rules had to be closely followed. No matter how much he wanted her to himself, he'd never ask her to move.

Another couple entered the model, and Lanier and Dallas regrouped then quickly exited. The man looked as if he recognized Dallas but said nothing.

Lanier giggled. "Did you see how hard that guy was staring at you?"

Dallas shrugged. "He was probably trying to place me."

Dallas's fame was merely a part of what he did for a living and nothing to do with who he was as a man. Some sports figures got caught up in the fame game, but not him. Dallas was grounded and he loved his fans and enjoyed meeting them. Superstar attitude was not in him.

Dallas grinned. "Houston's the ham in the family, and he loves his megastar power. He has settled down a lot down since meeting Kelly. She brought him down to earth in a hurry."

"She certainly tamed that big old Texas boy."

"Yeah, and my parents are totally gone on Kelly. I wonder when they'll walk down the aisle."

Lanier looped her arm through Dallas's. "They're smart not to rush into anything, even if they are perfect for each other."

Dallas outlined Lanier's heart with his finger. "Are we?"

Lanier shut her eyes. "Not as perfect as I want. It's on me, though. I have lots of imperfections. I want to give you my all, and I'm working hard to get it right."

Dallas frowned. "The last thing I want is for you to do hard labor in this relationship." If it didn't come to her naturally, he feared they'd never work as a couple. Thinking she might not love him enough to marry him was upsetting. Yet, deep down inside, he felt loved by her.

As the couple moved through the next town house, Dallas was quiet. His carefree mood had changed to more reserved. Lanier made him think hard and worry too much about what was happening inside her head, yet she was also the only one who could make changes in herself.

Dallas had no desire to change Lanier, but he wanted her to be totally confident about her feelings for him. Forcing a time frame on her wouldn't help, either. But he didn't plan to wait forever for her to make up her mind about loving him enough to marry. Perhaps she just couldn't love that hard. But there was no in-between for him; it was all or nothing.

As soon as they'd entered the last town house, Lanier perked up. "Oh, my goodness, look at this place. It's beautiful, the kind of home I've dreamed of! I know I haven't seen it all, but I love what I see."

Moving into the spacious kitchen, Lanier's hands lovingly swept the granite counters. That all appliances were stainless steel had her tickled pink.

"Look here, Dallas. An entire stainless package is standard instead of an upgrade."

Dallas grinned and grabbed her hand, steering her toward the wrought-iron staircase.

Lanier stopped on the stairway. Turning to Dallas, she cupped his face between her hands. "This is it! I feel it. I probably should look at a few more complexes, but I bet I'll end up right back here."

"This one really is great. Have you thought about buying instead of leasing? I can set you up with my Realtor. Just say the word and it's done."

"Maybe I will. I'm sure it's better to buy a home than pay rent and end up with nothing to show for it."

Lanier and Dallas rapidly made their way up the few remaining steps. They entered the master suite and the glowing expression on Lanier's face said it all. "How huge is this! Oh, my God, check out the bathroom with that fabulous tub. I can imagine us in it together."

Dallas could imagine it, too. The thought of Lanier straddling him in the tub caused a rise in his manhood. He made a mental note to coerce her into the bathroom Jacuzzi at his house.

Lanier's wild enthusiasm over the largest town house had Casey smiling. "I'll work up both sets of figures for you. If you finance with us, we pay closing costs and offer ten thousand dollars in upgrades."

Lanier looked hopeful. So many things rushing around in her brain suddenly made her feel off-kilter. Leasing or buying was a big step. Knowing she had excellent credit had her worry-free. If the price was right, Lanier was sure she could accomplish it.

Smiling, Lanier took Dallas's hand. His gentle squeeze was reassuring.

Lanier held up her forefinger. "One more question. Are the locations of leased homes and purchased homes mixed together in the same neighborhoods?"

Casey shook her head. "Purchased homes and leased

ones are set apart by brick perimeters. Security gates are provided at both entries."

Gathering up all paperwork related to the complex, Lanier shoved them in a manila folder Casey had given her. After shaking hands with the manager, she and Dallas were ready to go.

The moment they stepped out into the sunlight, Dallas brought her into his arms and kissed her thoroughly. "I guess I can tell you now."

Lanier hunched her shoulders. "Tell me what?"

Dallas laughed. "We fell in love with the same town house."

"I'm glad you approve. I felt the chemistry in spades. The rooms seemed to reach out and embrace me. The master suite has everything I could want. It wasn't my bed, but it was sure summoning me to try it out," she said, laughing. "My imagination got away from me in there."

Dallas kissed the tip of her nose. "Mine was right there with yours. I'm glad the air conditioner was on."

Lanier laughed. "I love it when we're on the same page."

Taking Lanier's hand in his, Dallas started walking toward the car. "It happens to us a lot." He glanced at his watch. "Let me get you back to Haven House so I can go home and lay down for a while. Resting before practice never hurts."

Envisioning him up to bat, Lanier swung their entwined hands back and forth. "I love to see your muscles ripple when you're on deck."

"In that case, I'll try to give you a real good show." He flexed his upper arm muscles. "Iron clad," he joked.

Lanier smiled. She loved his muscles and his strength, but she particularly loved how protected she felt nestled in his powerful arms.

Dallas had a hard time leaving Lanier's warm embrace. She had come into his arms as soon as they had entered the house. She was kissing him as if she couldn't get enough of his mouth, and he was returning her moist kisses with unbridled passion. Knowing this would probably end with him taking a cold shower, he still couldn't pull away. His manhood was stiff as a board, grinding up against her body with tender force.

Lanier loosened the buckle on his belt and then lowered his zipper. She wasn't in control of herself and she didn't care. Reaching inside his fly, she found his erection and began moving her closed hand up and down his shaft.

Losing his hands in her hair, he tugged gently. Tilting her head back, his tongue licked up and down her throat. Unbuckling her belt, he removed it and slid the slacks halfway off her hips. As his hands slid into her panties, she gasped wantonly. For only a fleeting moment she thought of where they were. She easily convinced herself that foreplay was not intercourse.

Continuing to pump her hands up and down his sex, she wrapped her hands around him tighter. Bringing him as much pleasure as she could was what was on her mind. She wanted to send him off to his nap with something hot and sweet to think about.

As Dallas's fingers probed inside of her, it was all

she could do to remain standing. She was wet and hot and he was hard as stone and his breathing was jagged. In the next instant, she felt the ripples of a powerful climax wending its way throughout her inner chamber. Dallas muffled both of their moans of fulfillment as he covered her mouth with his.

After kissing her breathless, he went into the downstairs bathroom and Lanier ran to the one upstairs.

Looking into the mirror, Lanier saw how glazed over her eyes looked. The color in her cheeks was heightened and her hair was all over the place from Dallas pushing his hands through it. She smiled, wishing he didn't have to leave, yet she was happy they'd both been satisfied.

Chapter 3

Lanier met with the rest of the Carrington family to watch the game. Lanier and Ashleigh embraced a long time. Once everyone had been accounted for, Beaumont and Austin led the way to the luxury box seats reserved for family and friends. While his parents tried hard not to miss a single game, there were times when they had to split up to ensure their sons had family support at their different games.

Leaning forward in her seat, Lanier kept her eyes on Dallas. Dallas was up to bat. His powerful physique had her wishing she could laze her hands over every muscle he had. Just the thought of it turned her on. "Go, baby. Send that ball into orbit."

The crowd was boisterous, and a low pitch was called as ball one. "Ouch," she soon yelped, grimacing at his first strike. A foul ball came next, giving Dallas two strikes and one ball. She stood and prayed for a hit.

The bat cracked loudly as it met with the speeding ball, which soared high and kept going. Everyone jumped up as the baseball flew into the stands.

"Poetry in motion," Lanier shouted. "You go, Dallas!"

Lanier jumped up and down, cheering as loud as she could. Dallas's home run had put his team ahead by two runs. The fourth inning was going the Hurricanes' way. Lanier wished for a victory, especially since Dallas loved to celebrate wins.

Not only was Dallas superromantic after a win, but he was extremely high-spirited. When they lost, he didn't take it out on anyone, but he wasn't happy. He took it personally when his team gave up a game, vowing to practice even harder. Like all Hurricanes fans, Lanier preferred a win over a loss, but she loved to be with Dallas either way.

As Dallas ran the bases, Lanier and Ashleigh high-fived.

Lanier had never had the privilege of sitting in any seat at a sporting event before she knew Dallas, let alone box seats. She had been lucky to get enough food to eat each day.

How many former foster children got to hang out with rich, superstar heroes?

Looking at Lanier adoringly, Dallas massaged lotion into her legs and feet, still excited that she had agreed to spend the night. Without the slightest hesitation, she had given him an answer to a question he'd feared asking. She had been eager to go home with him. He couldn't believe his good fortune.

Stretched out on the custom king bed in a sexy black gown, she felt red-hot and sexy.

Lanier stilled his hands. "The massage feels great, but I'm ready for the main event."

Taking in a deep breath, Dallas tried to calm his heart rate. "I love how you get straight to the point."

Lanier gave a soft, guttural growl and smiled devilishly. Taking the lotion from Dallas's hand, she set it on the nightstand. She urged him to come closer and then laid flat on her back. Placing her hand at his nape, she guided his head until it rested between her perky breasts. "What's your pleasure, superstar?" Lanier stroked his face. "Name it."

"What about boundaries?"

Her eyes gleamed flirtatiously. "Only those you put in force."

Managing to get Dallas flat on his back, Lanier straddled his powerful thighs, positioning her buttocks below his manhood. She smothered his chest with moist kisses and flicked his erect nipples with her tongue. Dallas moaned deeply.

Slowly, tantalizingly, she inched the silk boxers off his waist. His shaft, hardened by passion, came into view. Lanier sighed as white-hot desire washed over her in one scorching wave after another. "Can I have my way with you?"

"Anyway you choose. Baby, I'm all yours."

"Mmm, yummy." Her head dipped down again, going much lower than his chest.

As if sampling something she'd never had before, Lanier tasted the crown of his manhood. She pulled slightly back and licked her lips. Loving the thrill of it, she sampled him like a brand-new lollipop flavor. She lifted her head and looked him square in the eyes. "You taste good. Mind if I have more?"

Dallas locked eyes with hers—and he was stunned by this newfound provocativeness. Her mouth on his naked hardness felt insanely good. Fearing she might change her course of action, he didn't dare move a muscle. He'd been holding his breath in anticipation, but he let out a stream of ragged breathing. "I love it when you have your way. Take all you want." As her mouth curled around his manhood, he gasped. "Oh, yes," he moaned softly. "I want you to taste every part of me."

Lanier happily honored his breathless request. Her glance at him was fleeting, yet she saw how tightly he held his eyes shut, lost in his own pleasure.

Using the tip of her tongue, Lanier recircled the crown of his manhood and then began to lick him up and down. After kissing every inch of his erection, she sampled all of him, taking her sweet time giving him what he desired.

She loved roving his body with her mouth, lips and tongue. Lanier silently hoped he'd taste her, too.

As if Dallas felt Lanier's desire to have his mouth and tongue serenade her intimate zones, he raised himself. Rolling her away from him and turning her onto her back, he looked down and studied her beauty. He tenderly stroked her breasts with his fingertips and then seduced her with an intensely passionate kiss. "Now I'm going to have my way. I want you, Lanier, badly."

Lanier's eyelashes lowered. "I'm here, Dallas. Take me."

Sampling Lanier wasn't all Dallas had in mind. Preferring to take it nice and slow, his tongue cautiously teased and hotly tantalized her intimate treasures, his fingers working magic on her at the same time.

"Don't close your eyes. I want you to witness and feel everything." He lowered his head, slowly lapping his tongue between her legs.

Trying not to thrash about wildly, she tightly gripped the sheets, unable to believe the zinging sensations coursing through her burning flesh. "Dallas," she cried, "what are you doing to me?" She bit down on her lower lip. "Don't stop." Hot tears trickled from the corners of her eyes as Dallas's mouth continued to make her feel sensational.

All Lanier wanted was for Dallas to continue extinguishing the lake of fire burning out of control. Suddenly, her body arched wildly, uncontrollably. As rolling wave after wave of sensational fulfillment carried her away, she moaned helplessly.

Eager to be deep inside of her, Dallas managed to protect them and then entered her. As he rode the waves of ecstasy Lanier was already high on, Dallas had a hard time holding back his own release. Things had heated up for him much quicker than he'd expected. Pleasuring her had come first. It had been his desire to give her a sensual experience she'd never forget.

Unable to hold on another second, he tenderly plunged into her time after time, calling out her name as a firestorm of white-hot heat raced through his body.

Opening her eyes, Lanier scanned his gorgeous face, excited to see the telltale signs of his release. "You feel what I feel?"

"Every bit of it, babe, if incredible is what you're feeling."

"I'm way past that. I can't even appropriately name those foreign feelings. Thanks." She looked embarrassed. "I hope you're okay with the way I showed my love for you. It's not something I've done before, and I don't want you to think otherwise."

"Hush, sweetheart. I know who you are. Let's just think about us and how we make each other feel. There's no reason for embarrassment. We got it like that." He paused, appearing thoughtful. "There's something I should tell you."

Trembling inwardly, Lanier's left eyebrow lifted. "What?"

"What we're feeling is only the tip of the iceberg. I'm convinced there are more uncharted waters for us to navigate. We should enjoy every second of what we do together. Can you handle that?"

Lanier smiled softly. "I can." She tried to stifle a yawn and failed. The last thing she wanted to do was fall asleep. She had so much to stay awake for.

Dallas chuckled. "Looks like someone's sleepy."

Lanier frowned. "I can't fall asleep until you make love to me until I'm too tired to flex a single muscle."

Uninhibited wasn't a strong enough adjective to describe Lanier. She had transformed from a shy, sweet woman to this alluring, provocative tigress. Not for one second did he think it was anything other than spontaneous behavior. Whether she'd intended it or not, Lanier had exposed her heart and freed her inhibitions.

"I'd love to make nonstop love to you every day and

night. The condoms are in the nightstand drawer." His eyes gently caressed her. "I'm waiting."

Dallas was thoroughly intrigued by the Lanier he'd just been introduced to. He loved the old one, but if he had to make a choice between old and new, he couldn't decide, not without further introductions to the woman she desired to be.

Tearing her gaze from him, Lanier scooted across the mattress and opened the nightstand's top drawer. Pulling out a strip of condoms, she tore one away. Her eyes reconnected with Dallas's, boldly, soulfully.

Slowly, carefully, Lanier rolled a condom onto his rock-hard organ. She looked down, intently watching the movements of her own hands. Now that the latex was snugly in place, she sighed deeply. "The rest is up to you."

Wrapping Lanier tightly in his arms, Dallas kissed her face, neck and ears. "Why leave the rest to me? I love you being in control. Don't stop now."

Using her thumb, Lanier smoothed each of his brows. She had to smile. "Want me in control? I'm there."

Pushing Dallas back on the bed, Lanier mounted him, lowering herself down onto his hardened length. As her core vacuum sealed his erection, she clenched her inner muscles tighter, throwing back her head. The ecstasy steamrolling through her body was hard to bear. "Dallas," she whispered, "I'm in control...and loving it."

Dallas managed a moan. With Lanier seared onto his manhood, there was nothing he could do. Being inside her was heaven. As she moved atop him, bucking and jerking with wild abandon, he felt intense heat from inside her. Moisture rapidly pooled around his erection.

Placing both hands on her hips, he thrust upward, burying his sex deeper.

Starting to lose it, he quickly flipped her on her back. Cupping her face with his hands, he tenderly plunged his tongue in and out the warm recesses of her mouth. "You make me crazy, Lanier." As much as he liked her in control, he didn't want to go off prematurely. He'd last a lot longer on top.

Drawing her closer and closer, he made sure their bodies stayed perfectly aligned. Looking into her eyes, he couldn't help thinking of how much he loved her. This woman was unique, and he wanted her in every possible way. No one had ever captured his heart.

Austin was married and Houston was engaged. Dallas wanted what his brothers had. His desire for Lanier to totally surrender to their love kept him hoping for a miracle. If only she'd find enough courage to trust her fragile heart to him, Dallas knew he'd never break it.

Shutting off his mind, Dallas turned his full attention back to Lanier. Desiring to put all his energy into pleasing the woman lying beneath him, he captured her lips and kissed her ravenously.

Lanier's eyes sparkled with lust. "Give me everything you have."

"I don't want to deny you anything." He nipped at her lower lip with his teeth, kissing her deeply.

Lifting Lanier's buttocks, Dallas plunged deeper into her moistness. He gasped with pleasure as she clenched her inner muscles. Inch by inch, slowly and tenderly, he drove deeper into her.

Lanier did everything in her power to keep from digging her nails into Dallas's back. The man knew how to please her, and she was already at the brink of release. As Dallas's manhood executed another deep thrust, her eyes rolled back. Fighting hard to stay with him, desperately trying to keep up the frenzied pace, she lost herself to the heat waves.

"You feel so good inside me, Dallas." She moaned, arching into him. "I'm running out of time," she whispered shakily. "I'm about to explode."

Dallas was close to an explosion but unready to surrender. The end of the road loomed dead ahead and he sighed. "Ready to sail over the rainbow?"

"Please take me there…" Hoarsely, she screamed his name, salty tears cascading.

In the throes of an intense climax, Lanier's body shook tumultuously. Totally lost in a delicious euphoria, too worn out to try to prolong it, she let go and her body shook forcefully. Dallas joined her at the same time, experiencing the most body-jolting climax he'd ever had.

Rolling over and turning up on his side, Dallas looked down at Lanier. He expected her to jump up and run into the bathroom, telling him she had to shower and leave—a finale he wasn't fond of. Plumping his pillow, Dallas laid it close to Lanier and lowered his head and closed his eyes. As her breath fanned his cheek, he sighed.

It took Dallas several minutes to realize Lanier was fast asleep. Although he knew she'd want to be woken, he decided to let her rest. Looking at her beautiful face had him wanting to make love all over again. She was beautiful awake and in her sleep. He tried not to think about how disappointed he'd feel once she left.

Still not sure if she should wake her, Dallas's eyes continued roving her relaxed body. "Lanier, Lanier," he whispered, "I'm so in love with you. You have no idea how much you mean to me."

Lanier stirred and Dallas laid his head back on the pillow.

Leaning over Dallas, Lanier kissed him softly on the mouth. She laid her head on his chest and looked up at him, her fingernail tracing his bottom lip. She loved to see him so relaxed. He had to be dead tired from the ball game. Splaying her fingers over his chest, she closed her eyes. "I love you. Good night."

Waiting for her to get up and take flight, Dallas drew in a sharp intake of breath. He'd do just about anything to take her mind off leaving in the middle of the night.

Then Dallas heard Lanier's even breathing, surprised but pleased she'd fallen back to sleep. He smiled and wrapped her up in his arms.

Lifting her arms, Lanier stretched them and rolled her neck around to loosen the muscles. She couldn't remember the last time she had felt so completely rested. She had slept like the dead last night. Dallas's custom mattress must've been designed in heaven.

Usually she was so ridden with anxiety when she slept at Dallas's that she had trouble falling asleep. She normally went over the entire evening in her mind, trying to recall if she'd done everything right or if she might've said or done something stupid. This time had been different, and she'd relaxed enough to fall right off to sleep.

Lifting Dallas's pillow, Lanier inhaled his familiar scent. The clean and woodsy cologne smell clung to the linens. She could hear noises coming from somewhere in the house.

The only thing Lanier wore was a big smile on her mahogany face. As she swung her legs out of bed, Dallas strolled into the room. "There you are. I was coming to look for you. Have you been up long?"

Dallas came over to the bed and dropped down. He pulled Lanier onto his lap and looked into her eyes. He tenderly dragged his thumb over her bottom lip and then kissed her forehead and neck. "I haven't been up long. I had to make a couple of phone calls, so I went into my office to keep from disturbing you."

Lanier chuckled under her breath. "Hmm, my sleeping pill worked that good?"

Dallas grinned, tenderly kissing her lips. "Babe, you have no idea how well it worked. I have to start eating Wheaties again so I can keep up with you. You were fierce last night!"

She turned down her mouth. "Aren't I fierce all the time?"

Dallas chuckled. "You are. I love exercising your very full lips. There are women out there who pay thousands of dollars for a mouth you inherited naturally."

"There are a few physical attributes I'd pay for, too, if I had the means."

Dallas drew his head back sharply, surprised. "Like what?"

Lanier shrugged. "My nose is a tad too big, and I'd have my ears pinned back."

Dallas couldn't keep from laughing. "We definitely don't want to tamper with your nose. Girl, you have the nose of an African queen. As for your ears, who can see them with all the silky hair you have? Besides, pinned back or not, your ears hear me every time I say I love you, even when I whisper. Your nose and ears are fine. Everything about you is exactly how it should be."

Smiling, Lanier blushed. "You're the only one who says the most beautiful and meaningful things to me... and makes me believe them."

Dallas smiled and nodded. "There is a saying and a song that applies perfectly to me. *Fools rush in.* I love rushing into everything to do with you and me. I didn't intend to rush love. I had no choice. Love rushed me. And I'm glad you stopped running away."

Lanier's heart filled with love for Dallas. "I'll leave my features alone, then. Thanks for loving me as I am." No one but Dallas had ever made her feel so beautiful. Her expression suddenly grew somber and she nervously chewed on her lower lip. "About the song you just mentioned—it had a ring of truth. Sometimes I feel like a fool rushing in. It feels like we're rushing commitment. Do you ever get that feeling?"

Dallas's eyes widened. Her comment had stung him. "I don't like the sound of that. If you feel like a fool, why do you stay in this relationship?"

His tone bothered her. Upsetting him hadn't been her intent. "You're twisting my words."

He shrugged. "How can that be? They were plain as day."

"Maybe so, but you're taking them out of context, Dallas."

"Then you tell me what you meant. I don't want to get it twisted."

She picked up a pillow. "I don't know what I meant. I shouldn't have said it."

"You said it because it's how you feel, Lanier."

"And it obviously offended you. Can we change the subject?"

Dallas was frustrated. Lanier's take on things didn't make sense to him. "No, it just made me wonder why you'd stay around if you feel rushed. It's been three years. You feel rushed and I feel like our relationship is in a holding pattern. That's what's obvious to me."

"Sorry you feel that way." Ready to flee, Lanier stood. "Maybe we shouldn't see each other until you're clear on what it is you want from me?"

"I know what I want," he yelled. "For starters, clarity would be nice!"

Lanier rushed past Dallas and ran into the bathroom, shutting the door behind her.

Dallas wanted to slam his fist into the door, but he pulled back. It would serve no purpose and only cause destruction to his property. "You're not going to be able to dodge bullets forever. At some point, you'll have to open up and let everything come out."

After such a beautiful evening, the morning wasn't going very well. He knew this conversation on her feeling rushed into commitment was over. Lanier had a knack for clamming up when serious issues arose, especially the ones she didn't want to deal with.

* * *

Dallas looked up as Lanier came back into the bedroom. He wasn't completely over the earlier episode, but he may as well have been. Lanier would simply refuse to revisit the issue. "What about some breakfast? I can mix up a batch of my silver-dollar pancakes you love so much and grill us some sausages."

Lanier's palm went to her bare stomach. "Sounds divine, but I can't help overeating the pancakes. A piece of toast and hot tea will do the trick."

Dallas walked over to Lanier and kissed her. "Coming right up. Want to eat in here or in the kitchen?"

Lanier pointed at the French doors. "Let's eat in here where we can see the pool area."

Dallas nodded. "We'll eat in here. Be back in a jiffy."

Lanier sighed. As she tried to restore the peace she'd felt earlier, she looked around the room. Although she was happy that Dallas seemed as if he was over the disagreement, she knew there'd come a time he'd demand answers. He didn't like confrontation, but there was a lot they had to get out in the open. She was sorry she'd voiced to him how she sometimes felt.

Dallas walked back into the bedroom and looked around for Lanier. After setting down the tray on the round table, he went into the bathroom. He watched how tenderly she touched her body in the shower. How she washed herself was provocative.

Smiling, Dallas backed quietly out of the room. He was happy she was comfortable enough to shower in his home. He saw it as a good sign because this was another first for her.

Since she only had the clothes she'd worn last evening, Dallas went into the massive walk-in closet to retrieve them. He removed her attire from hangers to take to her.

Lanier came into the bedroom at the same time Dallas exited the closet. He sucked in a deep breath. Beads of water clung to her baby-soft skin, and he had an overwhelming desire to dry off her fabulous body with his tongue. In an attempt at taking his eyes and mind off her nude body, he went into the bathroom linen closet and retrieved an oversize towel.

Dallas wrapped the towel around Lanier's body. "How were you going to dry off if I hadn't come back?"

Lanier shrugged. "I knew where the towels were. I came to get my clothes, but you already have them. You're so thoughtful." She looked adoringly at him. "Well, are you planning to dry me off or not? It *is* getting a little chilly."

Dallas began drying her off. Although he wanted them to enjoy their breakfast—staring into her soulful eyes, staring into her—he also desperately desired an encore. Dallas had it bad for Lanier, and he wasn't totally sure if it was good for him.

Chapter 4

Lanier looked out the kitchen window and thought of how summer was quietly slipping away. Fall was fast approaching. After pouring two mugs of French roast coffee, she carefully carried them over to the table and handed one to Ashleigh, and then sat down. "How did A.C. sleep last night?"

"He had us up until the wee hours of the morning." Ashleigh laughed. "Fortunately for us, he wasn't sick. He's just an absolute chatterbox."

"He's a good baby," Lanier remarked. "Remember how the girls used to want to stay up all night to tell us lots of bedtime stories? But they were always careful not to give away one another's secrets."

"Yeah, they were excellent at keeping secrets. We still haven't found out the name of the guy Tina had a crush on…and it's been months since we learned she had a crush."

Ashleigh took a sip of her coffee. "We know it wasn't her prom date. She says he's only a good friend."

"It's definitely not him." Lanier drummed her fingers on the table. "With all the guys she's met lately, we may never find out who she had her eye on."

"You're probably right." Ashleigh smiled. "What did you and big D get into after the game last week? Or maybe I should ask what you two came out of, unless it's a secret."

Lanier grinned. "Girl, you need to stop. I'm not a secret keeper. I learned the hard way how dangerous secrets can be. I've heard it said that we're only as sick as our secrets. If I hadn't kept quiet about what went on in our home, my parents may've gotten help a lot sooner."

Ashleigh hated hearing Lanier still blame herself for her parents' issues. "You were only a child then. You kept it a secret because you thought they'd go to jail. I thought you'd finally gotten past it all."

Lanier blinked repeatedly. "Let me get back to your original question. We had a magnificent evening after the game. I fell asleep on him and actually spent the whole night. I wish I'd been able to see the look on his face when I didn't get up and run home."

"Dallas knows how you feel about staying out all night. We're both guilty of acting like the girls are still here, but next month they'll leave for college. We'll get new kids, but it was smart of us to take time off before the upcoming school year. By the way, what have you decided about the town house?"

Lanier wrinkled her nose. "The decision is more about buying versus leasing. I've already filled out the loan application just in case, and I have a copy of the lease agreement if I go that way."

"I can understand that. But don't you think you'd need the same amount of credit whether you lease or purchase?"

Lanier stood. "Probably so, but let me worry about it. I don't want you to stress over anything involving me."

"Okay, but you know I'm always here to help," said Ashleigh.

Lanier nodded. "Thanks."

"Now that we've settled the town house issue," Ashleigh said, "let's tackle our monthly expenses for the business. We also need to discuss plans for taking in new kids."

Lanier nodded. "Let's get started. It's your turn to write checks."

Ashleigh laughed. "I don't know anyone who hates writing checks as much as you. You know, our finances are in great shape. We don't have to worry about money like we used to."

"Thanks for the reminder." Lanier smiled.

Dallas unsealed a note-size envelope, finding it odd that there was no return address. But it had been post-marked in Houston. His address was written in a beau-tifully hand-printed calligraphy.

As he removed a small sheet of pink linen statio-nery, a heavenly scent gently tickled his nostrils. He put the paper up to his nose and inhaled to get a stronger whiff. Unable to identify the scent, he began perusing the note.

Dear D.C.:
Just a short note to let you know that I'm a secret
admirer and that I plan to reveal my identity in the
near future. I know you have millions of female
fans, but no one can give you what I have to offer.
If you liked the smell of the scented paper, you
may like it better on me. To tell you a little about
myself, I'm into fulfilling fantasies, role-playing
and hot men like you. I have many wonderful attributes, but I want you to discover them on your
own. I hope this note intrigues you as much as
I'm captivated by you. And be on the lookout for
my next correspondence. It'll be sent within the
next few days.

In each note you'll be given some juicy tidbit to
make you look forward to receiving the next one.
I know you're seeing someone, but you'll forget
about her. I hope you enjoy this sexy game of intrigue. It has only just begun.
Ciao!

Dallas reread the note three times before inserting it
back into the envelope. He wondered how the mystery
writer had gotten hold of his home address. All types of
letters and gifts were received at the postal boxes that
the team management provided for fan mail. This was
the first personal note that had been delivered to his
home.

Someone he didn't know knew where he lived. It
was a big deal to him. He sniffed at the envelope again
and confirmed that it didn't smell like any scent Lanier
wore. His secret admirer didn't pass the smell test.

Dallas laid the letter on the glass coffee table and then walked into the master bedroom. He immediately picked up a stunning photograph of him and Lanier. He sat on the nearby chaise and looked at the photo, recalling their last passionate rendezvous of a week ago. He used a fingertip and traced the lips of the sweetest mouth he couldn't get enough of.

The ringing doorbell interrupted his sentimental mood. Agitated, he got up. After carefully setting the picture on the dresser, he walked rapidly toward the front, wondering who the visitor was. It had to be someone that security had permitted to enter his estate.

Dallas snatched the door open and saw Houston on the porch. They gave each other a warm hug and a hard slap on the back. "Come on in. I was about to lie down and take a short nap. Can I get you something to eat or drink?"

Houston shook his head. "Thanks, but no thanks. I only stopped by for a minute." Following Dallas into the family room, Houston took a seat on the leather sofa. "I need your advice on something."

Dallas pointed at his ears. "They're open and available."

Houston wrung his hands together. "I thought about what I wanted to say all the way over here, now I can't seem to get it out…"

Dallas looked concerned. "Are you okay physically? What is it?"

"No, man, it's nothing like that. My physical health is A-1. Not so sure about my mental state, though. This is so crazy, but I'm a little worried about my relationship with Kelly."

"Why are you so concerned? Did something bad happen between you two?"

"It's about our engagement. Believe it or not, I can't pin her down on a wedding date. Everything in my personal life has changed drastically. I ran away from Kelly before, and now I find myself running to her every chance I get."

Dallas checked a chuckle. "What happens when you mention setting a date?"

"She sort of brushes me off, saying we have plenty of time to set a date."

"Maybe she wants to make sure you're ready to settle down." Dallas laughed. "You weren't an easy catch, you know. You gave her a run for her money."

Houston began to relax. "You guys just won't let me forget that, will you?"

"Not anytime soon. But when you fell, you sure fell hard for her." Dallas paused for a moment. "I'm sorry. This isn't something to joke about. Do you think Kelly may've changed her mind about marrying you?"

Houston shrugged. "I don't know. The subject seems to scare her all of a sudden. I'm asking for straight answers, but I can't get any. Maybe I need to stop bringing it up."

Dallas pressed his lips together. "Maybe you're overreacting. She accepted your proposal and she's been with you ever since your first date. Unless she tells you she doesn't want to get married, back off."

"Just like you've been doing with Lanier, huh?"

Dallas grabbed his stomach. "Ouch! That was a hard blow, man! Lanier is not wearing a diamond engagement ring. She may never wear mine. But I don't hand out ultimatums to anyone. I'll wait awhile longer."

Houston raised an eyebrow. "How *much* longer?"

"As long as it takes for me to realize marriage isn't in our future. Love can't be turned on and off like a faucet. I love her, Houston. I love her more than I can express."

Houston's ebony eyes softened. "I know you do, man. Lanier certainly looks at you like she loves you. Does she tell you how she feels?"

"All the time. I blame most of her fears on the dysfunction within their family. She only recently met with her estranged parents. She hadn't seen or talked to them in years."

Houston moved to the edge of his seat. "How'd it go?"

"I was surprised at how well it went down. Lanier showed a lot of courage. But growing up in foster homes left her terribly vulnerable. I'm not sure she believes I'm in this relationship for life."

"After hearing what you had to say, I'll stop pushing Kelly. She's had issues with her parents, too. I haven't bombarded her with specific wedding dates, but I have shown impatience over her lack of interest in discussing it." Houston stood. "I'm glad I came out here to talk. Austin wasn't home, and Ashleigh was at Haven House for a business meeting with Lanier."

"Preseason started for Austin a couple of weeks ago." Dallas said. "He probably wants to spend as much time as possible with A.C. before his travel schedule gets really crazy. But, before we know it, spring training will roll around again. I hope we go back to camp as winners of the World Series. We're so close."

"Man, I pray that your team gets to the big show. There's nothing sweeter than winning."

Houston walked over to the window and looked out. "I wonder if Kelly has changed her mind about making a life with me. She's superbusy these days, and sometimes I feel like I need to make an appointment to see her. Her patients are her top priority. I feel like she has me on a back burner."

"You know better than that." Dallas walked over to Houston and put his hand on his shoulder. "She's a dedicated physician, little brother. There are doctors out there that don't put a lot of care into their patients. Kelly isn't one of them. Don't you want her to be the best at what she does?"

Houston frowned. "Of course I want that. I'm proud of her. At first I was happy she wouldn't travel with the team. It didn't take me long to change my mind. Is it wrong for me to want her to travel with me when she has a thriving medical practice? The thought of life on the road without her scares the hell out of me. I keep wondering when we'll find time for each other. I hope I'm not making too much of this."

"It's okay to be concerned, but whatever you do don't let Kelly know you're scared. Wait until your season gets underway and see how it goes. Don't put the cart before the horse."

"I know what you mean." Houston let out a sigh of relief. "If anyone had told me I'd be sweating a woman, I'd call them a liar. I feel like I've turned into a pansy."

Dallas laughed. "Oh, stop it, Houston. You're the same tough jock who scores a zillion points a game.

Give yourself a break. Kelly isn't going anywhere, and I'm sure she still plans to walk down the aisle with you."

"If not, I wish she'd tell me. I know Kelly wouldn't play with my heart, but I wonder if I'm setting us up to fail. She's the only woman I've ever fallen in love with."

"Keep on loving her, Houston. It's not like you two have been engaged for years. Give her space. It can't hurt."

"Thanks for the sound advice. The next time we see each other will be at my house for dinner. By the way, your last game was great! You always manage to come up with the clutch hit."

"Just like you manage to hit all those buzzer-beaters. We're winners. Dad and Mom pounded perseverance and excellence into our heads. They talked, and fortunately, for all of us, we listened."

Houston smiled. "You can say that again. I can't imagine where we'd be without Mom and Dad."

"I don't even want to." Dallas thought about the letter. Picking up the envelope from the table, he handed it to Houston. "Want you to read this note I received in the mail."

As Houston read the letter, Dallas watched his brother's expressions, laughing inwardly when both his eyebrows shot up. It was a nice letter if both parties knew each other, Dallas mused. Since he didn't know the person, it was strange and possibly dangerous.

"Man, this chick is really coming on to you, even knowing that you're seeing someone. Maybe the note is from a dude," Houston joked.

Dallas glared at Houston. "Don't even play like that.

It was sent to the house instead of the postal box. Think I should be worried?"

"I would be. If you didn't give anyone your personal address, you should be damn worried. Thank God you live behind security gates. No one can sail in and out of here at will."

"Close friends know where I live, so someone could've possibly gotten the address that way. Then again, I don't think they'd give it out."

Houston nodded. "It looks like this is just the first note of more to come. You think Lanier sent it?"

"No way! She wouldn't let me think I'm in danger."

"Keep a close eye on whatever you get in the mail. Maybe there'll be some sort of clue to an identity. Be careful, man." Houston looked at his watch. "I'm out of here. See you at dinner next week." Houston hugged his brother and left, more concerned about Dallas than he'd let on.

A thoughtful expression on his face, Dallas sat back down. Houston was the last person he'd ever thought would have woman trouble. Going to Kelly with any of Houston's concerns wasn't an option. Dallas knew he'd have to wait until the couple solved it between them. *Unless...*

The jangle of the phone redirected Dallas's attention and he answered the call. Hearing Lanier's voice made him smile. The slight huskiness of her tone warmed him. "Hey, you, what's going on?"

"You," Lanier countered. "I miss you and called to hear your sexy voice. Are you free this evening?"

Dallas was astonished. Lanier never asked him to spend time with her; usually he had to initiate their dates. Well, she had asked him to attend the luncheon meeting with her parents and to view the town houses, he recalled. He loved the demure Lanier and the deeply passionate woman only he got to see. She was becoming a lot more outgoing and bubbly.

"As a matter of fact, I *am* free. Have something specific in mind?"

Lanier grinned. "Oh, boy, do I! How does seven o'clock sound?"

"Anytime is fine with me. Can I bring something?"

"Your sexy body…and a voracious appetite. I plan to fix dinner."

"Sounds pretty delicious to me. Are you featured on the dessert menu?"

Laughter trilled from Lanier's throat. "I can be. Let me see. What dessert best describes me? What about a fudge brownie, dark and delectable, fresh out the oven?"

Dallas laughed. "Hmm, I think you got something there. Since you're a tad crazy, nuts should be added to the mix before baking."

"I like that," she said, giggling. "A warm fudge brownie with nuts sounds heavenly."

Dallas laughed again. "What've you been doing?"

"Ashleigh just left. We talked more about expansions for Haven House. I finally let her set up bill-pay on my computer. I hate writing checks."

Lanier went on to tell Dallas that she and Ashleigh were thinking of taking in emergency placements. "I was an emergency placement. With all the land we own, we're considering adding on a larger dining room and a couple more bedrooms."

"I know you and Ash want to help as many kids as possible."

"The social service department knows we'll have vacant beds come mid-September. But we won't take in new kids until the girls are off to college."

"The next group bound for Haven House will be lucky. You and Ashleigh are excellent foster parents."

"Thanks, Dallas. Glad you see how much we care for our kids. I have to go now. I've got some grocery shopping to do, and…" She refrained from telling him she was dropping off her credit application. "See you this evening."

"I can hardly wait. Love you."

"Love you, too." Lanier cradled the phone.

Grabbing her purse off the table, she went out to the garage. The town house complex was her first stop. If she waited any longer, she might not get it all done.

Dallas stared down at the phone, wondering more about this new Lanier. She had changed in ways he wouldn't have expected. The entire night she'd spent in his bed and in his arms still had his adrenaline pumping…and more than a week had passed.

Lanier could get way ahead of herself at times. Then she'd end up a bit depressed. He didn't want her to get like that again. Comebacks were so tough on her because she was treated very badly by a couple of foster families. It was one thing to be abandoned by your own parents, but it was worse to have new families treat you unkindly. No one completely changed overnight, and he clearly saw her efforts. Dallas loved her as she was.

He'd take her anyway he could get her, a testament to how much he truly loved her.

Dallas got up from the sofa and headed to the bedroom. Spotting his mail carrier leaving, he turned around and went outside to collect his mail. He opened the front door and stepped out.

Another pink envelope was in the stack of mail. Instead of waiting until he got back into the house, he ripped it open and immediately put the linen paper up to his nose. A totally different scent was on this note. It smelled like roses.

Dallas lifted his head and looked down after the government vehicle.

Could Tamara Hal, his mail carrier, be writing the notes?

Tamara had never given him any evidence to think she was hot for him, so he tossed the question out of his mind. They had flirted innocently a time or two, way before he'd met Lanier. Now they were merely friendly.

Then Dallas remembered the sweet-potato pie Tamara had brought to the door on Thanksgiving. A nice and thoughtful gesture, he surmised. Nothing out of the ordinary had happened, especially in the way of romance.

Dallas reached the porch and sat on the top step to read the note.

Hi, Dallas:
Hope you're fine. I watched you on television during the last game. I nearly went berserk when you hit the home run to put the Hurricanes ahead. It's hard to keep my eyes off you. That's how hot

you are. I miss a lot of action in the game because
I'm too busy watching you. I love your sexy swag-
ger. You're where all the action is. I can't imagine
what the team would do without their brightest!

I'd be happy if I knew you enjoyed the scent
on the envelopes. It is not perfume. I rubbed fresh
rose petals over the paper once I finished. This is
just a short note to say hello. I still plan to meet
you soon. I hope you'll be ready when I show up,
'cause I'm more than ready for you.

Ciao!

Dallas didn't understand this crazy mystery woman,
and he had no desire to meet her. This mess was getting
pretty scary for him. And Lanier was the only one he
wanted a lifetime with.

Casey scanned Lanier's application. "Everything
appears to be in order. We'll run a credit check and a
reference check will take place later. Because you're
self-employed, we'll need your tax returns for the past
two years."

"I only pay half the bills at Haven House. Will that
be taken into consideration? My business partner and I
split everything."

"I'm sure it will. Don't worry. If we run into problems, I'll let you know as soon as possible."

Lanier got to her feet. "Thanks, Casey. I appreciate
the help you've given me."

"It's been a pleasure for me, Lanier. How's Mr. Carrington?"

"He's fine. I'll tell him I finally turned in the application, after pondering it for weeks."

Casey closely eyed Lanier. "Are you two serious?"

Lanier was surprised by the question and more surprised by the way it was asked. "We're exclusive, if that's what you mean. Dallas and I met on a Valentine's Day cruise quite a while back."

Casey arched an eyebrow. "No marriage proposal?"

Lanier sucked in a deep breath. "We're fine the way things are."

Casey smirked. "He's an athlete, honey, a rich, successful one. Are you saying you're fine with him having a woman in every city he visits?"

Lanier ran a finger over her lower lip. "Your questions and remarks are personal...and I don't like them. Stick to selling townhomes."

With that said, Lanier walked out. She no longer cared if she qualified for the loan or not if it meant enduring the likes of Casey Rayburn.

Lanier shifted the car into Reverse and slowly backed out of the spot and drove out of the complex gates. She loved the town house, but she refused to deal with the kind of person she'd just encountered. Lanier made up her mind to ax the complex if anything like this happened again.

Chapter 5

Lanier rushed around the kitchen to check on the spaghetti sauce she was simmering. Dallas loved her recipe for his favorite pasta dish, which she'd gotten from an Italian woman in one of the neighborhoods she'd resided in. She had always liked to cook, finding peace in preparation. Whenever she was upset, working in the kitchen was calming.

Dallas smelled delightful to Lanier. The new cologne she had given to him suited him. He always smelled good to her, but there was something about the new fragrance that had her nuzzling her nose against his neck.

Dallas gently kissed Lanier and then handed to her a medium-size brown-paper-wrapped package. "Hope you like it," he said.

Smiling, her heart pumping fast, she went over to the sofa and sat down. After carefully situating the package on the coffee table, she ripped off the wrapping. "Oh, my goodness, it's a picture of us! It's beautiful. The frame is exquisite. When and where?"

Dallas grinned. "Look at it closely. I think you'll remember."

Her eyes suddenly lit up. "It's from formal night on your mother's birthday cruise! But you didn't take any pictures of us."

Dallas sat down next to her. "Ashleigh was taking pictures all over the place. I saw this photo at their house after we got back. She let me borrow the memory card to get a print made. I finally found time to get the photo enlarged and framed. I had one done for you, too."

Lanier gave Dallas a passionate kiss, loving this man whether she deserved him or not. No one made her feel the way he did. She stared into his eyes. "I love you, Dallas Carrington." *I'll never stop loving you.*

Dallas swallowed the lump in his throat. "If you ever try to tell me otherwise, I won't listen. I love you, too, Lanier Watson, and don't ever forget it. If you do, this picture should remind you of the kind of deep love we share."

"I won't forget." The moment had gotten a little too serious. Dallas's profound honesty still scared her at times. "Neither one of us can live off love, so I'll get dinner on the table. I popped bread into the oven before I let you in." Nerves jangling, she ran from Dallas's presence.

Disturbed by her fleeing, Dallas shoved his hand through his hair. He had to stop trying to make Lanier see their love as he saw it. It'd do her no good until she saw it with her own eyes. Knowing he shouldn't leave her alone with doubts running through her head, he rose and headed for the kitchen.

Dallas walked into the room and stood quietly for a moment, watching Lanier as she disappeared into the adjoining dining room. He picked up a bowl of tossed salad and a tray of hot bread and carried the items to the dining room. He saw that the table had been set beautifully.

Lanier came up beside him. "Thanks, Dallas. I'll get the rest. Sit down and relax." She turned to leave. Stopping suddenly, she whipped around to face him. "Wine, red or white?"

His smile was tender. "You choose. I want what you're having."

She smiled back. "Okay. I'll grab the casserole and a bottle of red wine."

Lanier came through the door and he jumped up, taking a hot serving dish from her hand and setting it on the table. He pulled out a chair for her and they both sat. Lanier gave a short blessing.

Lanier began fixing his plate. He didn't ask it of her, but he normally let it go without comment. She hadn't learned how much of a true caretaker she was until after the girls had moved in. Her own childhood had made it impossible to believe she'd become a great caretaker for others. Figuring Dallas was hungry, Lanier hurried. The sauce and pasta had been mixed together and then simmered on a low flame, the way he liked it.

Lanier watched while Dallas practically shoved food down his throat. She wasn't as eager to share the news as she'd been before seeing Casey. Before saying anything about the town house, she'd wait until he was on his second helping.

Dallas looked at Lanier and smiled. "Did you get your errands taken care of?"

"Pretty much. I also turned in a credit application for the town house." She sat back and waited on his response.

Dallas's eyes widened. "Congratulations!"

"I can't believe I actually followed through. Once I made up my mind to go for it, I tried not to second-guess myself. They need my tax returns, and I plan to take them by there tomorrow."

Thinking about how Casey acted, she pulled a face. "Maybe I'll mail them in."

"Why the ugly face? Did something bad happen?"

Lanier shrugged. "Just don't like people in my business."

"That's part of the loan process. They have to know about your employment and credit history. They don't ask only you for that information—everybody gets screened."

Lanier wrinkled her nose. "It wasn't that kind of information. Miss Rayburn decided to ask personal questions. I told her she needed to stick to her job and stay out of my personal life. She ticked me off."

Dallas laid down his fork and took Lanier's hand. "What in the world did she ask?"

"She wanted to know if we are in a serious relationship. I said we'd been together awhile, and she made a rude comment about an athlete's inability to be faithful."

Dallas's expression darkened. "You told her right.

She needs to stick to selling and leasing. Maybe I'll have a talk with the management, because she has no right to say anything about your personal business."

Lanier raised an eyebrow. "If she had her way, I'd probably be disqualified. She is in control. She seems to want what she thinks I have."

Dallas's eyes narrowed. "Thinks? Don't you know what you have?"

Lanier heard dismay in his voice. "I have you, Dallas. I have your heart and your love. I didn't mean to sound iffy."

Sighing, he smiled through the disappointment. "Those are the things I don't want you to forget. We'll pay Miss Rayburn a little visit tomorrow to deliver the tax returns."

Lanier shook her head. "I can handle her on my own. If she thinks I need you to fight my battles, she'll see me as weak. This is something I've got to deal with alone."

Impressed, Dallas nodded. "I'll stay out of it. But if she gives you a hard time, I'll have to deal with her."

"Don't worry, love. I've got it."

Dallas grinned. "I'm sure." He picked up his fork and resumed eating. His food had cooled some, but it still tasted delicious.

"Let me warm this up and what's left in the casserole," Lanier said as she took his plate into the kitchen with her.

Watching the door like a hawk, Dallas anxiously waited for Lanier. The room was cold without her warmth. Some folks would think he was a fool for love. He couldn't remember when he last cared about what people thought, especially about his feelings for his woman.

Fool or not, he was in love. Before Lanier, all he'd ever dreamed of was World Series wins. He'd forgo all of it to have Lanier marry him and live happily ever after.

Smiling, Lanier came through the door and set Dallas's plate before him. "It's piping hot. Be careful."

He pointed at her chair. "Sit back down and eat some more."

"I'm full. You eat as much as you want, but don't overdo it. I've got plans for you that require you to stay awake."

"I don't know what you have in mind, but my imagination is already going wild."

"Up to taking a walk with me?"

"Trying to help me work off the food I downed?"

"Just want to walk hand in hand. It's a beautiful evening."

It was a beautiful evening. A full moon shone its subtle light on the large tract surrounding Haven House. The atmosphere was peaceful. She felt alive with her hand inside Dallas's massive one. Every time he touched her, her pulse raced. As he leveled his dreamy, ebony eyes on her, she felt her knees weaken.

Dallas gently squeezed her hand. "I love how peaceful it is. I've lost track of the times we've walked this property, enjoying the atmosphere, losing ourselves in each other." His eyes drank in her beauty. "Are you okay?"

Lanier laid her hand on the side of his face. "I'm fine.

When I'm with you, I feel so much joy. I love it when we spend special times together, times like this."

Pulling her closer, Dallas kissed her forehead. "I love it, too, Lanier. I can't compare love, because you're my first. I was looking for something, but I didn't always know what I was searching for. Yet I knew love when I faced it the first time. And now I'm happier than I've ever been."

The couple fell into silence, walking on and enjoying the sounds of nightfall and rustling leaves. As Dallas looked over the property, he recalled how horrible Haven House had been before he, Houston and Austin had worked to turn a neglected place into a real home.

Lanier looked up at Dallas. "What're you thinking?"

Dallas chuckled. "The mess Haven House was before everyone went to work on it. The changes are remarkable."

"Ashleigh and I never dreamed the place could look this good, but we were determined to make it beautiful and as livable as possible."

"Mission accomplished." He pointed upward. "There's the North Star. Let's close our eyes and make a wish on it."

Lanier's wish was for more kids to keep Haven House filled with love, peace and joy.

"I'd love to tell you my wish, but it won't come true if I do," Dallas remarked.

"I won't try and persuade you to reveal it. I can't tell you mine, either. We both want our wishes to come true."

Stopping, Dallas turned to face Lanier, bringing her

into his arms. Lowering his head, he kissed her passionately.

"I'll race you to the gazebo." Laughing, Lanier took off running.

Hot on her heels, Dallas ran at top speed to catch her. He could overtake her anytime he wanted to, but he was happy with the view from behind. Her laughter floated back at him. No one laughed like Lanier. Blindfolded, he could pick out her melodic laughter in a crowded room.

Reaching the white gazebo, Lanier took Dallas's hand and they walked up the few steps. They situated themselves comfortably on the bench seating and then peered up at the ceiling. Countless tiny white and blue lights had been strung above a mural of black angels dressed in white, pink and blue robes and positioned on fluffy white clouds. Austin had paid an artist to do the intricate ceiling painting. Ashleigh loved angels, and he loved making her happy.

Dallas got up, walked over to a metal box and flipped on several light switches. A romantic blue-and-white light flooded the gazebo. As he hit another switch, soft music came on.

Dallas walked back to Lanier and extended his hand. "May I have this dance?"

Lanier got to her feet, allowing Dallas to lead her to the center of the floor. Floating into his strong arms, she wrapped hers about his neck and laid her head against his chest. "Does it get any better than this?"

"Our relationship can always get better. I want our love affair to be the best it can be. I think there's much more in store for us."

Dallas waltzed Lanier over the floor in a formal fashion. The instrumental music was slow and melodramatic, and the sounds from reeds and flutes were distinct.

"Back in the day, you'd wear a formal gown with rustling petticoats beneath and a corset-style waistline showing plenty of cleavage. I can imagine you wearing a half mask made of feathers, like something worn at a Mardi Gras ball. If any man tried to cut in, I'd tell him you're only eligible to me then I'd sweep you away."

Lanier laughed. "Is that so? You sound pretty sure of yourself."

Dallas looked her dead in the eyes. "Is there a reason I shouldn't be?"

Lanier winked at her charming dance partner. "No reason at all. I wish I had as much confidence as you. How is it you're always so sure of yourself?"

"I know who I am, inside and out, but I'll always be a work in progress. We're students of life until the day we die."

Unlike Dallas, Lanier was still learning who she was. She knew herself a lot better than she had a few years ago, but she was still growing. "You're one confident man. I love that about you. Where does it come from?"

"Mom and Dad deserve a good deal of the credit. The rest comes from life's trials and errors. When we make mistakes, we're supposed to learn from them, but we don't always. If we learn to weed the good from the bad, we won't settle for mediocre."

Lanier shook her head in dismay. "I've lost count of all the mistakes I've made." She sighed. Mistrusting everyone she came into contact with and everything she heard had been a huge problem for her. She was always suspicious of other's motives. Not believing in herself had to also be counted. Lanier still believed her biggest mistake had been calling 911 the night her parents had gotten into a terrible fight.

"Before I halfway figured it out, I was a repeat offender. I now know how to come away with a valuable lesson learned. I only wish I hadn't made the mistakes to begin with."

Dallas entwined his fingers in her hair. "It's okay to make mistakes, Lanier. We're only human. Gleaning something worthwhile from our experiences is important. I've been confident a long time, but cockiness never suited me. I had to learn how to show confidence without acting cocky."

Leading Lanier back to the bench, Dallas stood until she'd reclaimed her spot. "What is your biggest mistake?"

Lanier didn't have to give any thought to Dallas's query. "Calling 911 that night tops everything. Taking the blame for what others did is my second-worst mistake. I repeated that one again and again. Every time I got evicted from a house and sent to another, I owned the blame when I wasn't really to blame. Adults are supposed to be so much wiser than children, yet they make a mistake a minute. Isn't it funny how a child blames herself whenever someone is cruel to her?"

He hugged her. "Children are never to blame for what grownups do. They do mean things because they're plain evil or terribly frustrated with their own lives. Adults are supposed to teach the young, not berate them verbally and physically. As sweet as you are, I can't imagine anyone being mean to you. Wish I'd been around to protect you."

Lanier laughed. "My sweetness doesn't fool you. I can be pretty mean, and you're not a stranger to that part of me. But I'm actually guilty of being meaner to myself."

"You do whatever you have to do to protect yourself. I've never thought of you as mean, but your frustration can be plain as day. How's the new you progressing?"

Lanier raised both eyebrows. "I'm surprised you don't already know. Progression is going great. The old me would've told Casey where to go and how to get there. Though I did speak my mind, I was calm and direct."

Dallas cracked up. "Lucky her! She deserved to see you angry."

"I said it before—she wants what I have." Lanier gauged his reaction.

Dallas's smile was engaging. "And what's that?"

"You! She'd love to show you off to her family and friends. The woman is infatuated with a certain baseball player. I may have to buy you a T-shirt to stake my claim."

"Oh, yeah. What will it say?"

"My heart is taken!"

He laughed. "I'd wear it proudly."

Lanier yawned. "Excuse me. I'm getting sleepy. Must be all the food I ate."

"Girl, you didn't eat enough to keep a mouse alive. I'm the one who pigged out." He got to his feet. "Come on. Let me get you back to the house. It's getting late."

Dallas desperately wanted to ask Lanier to go home

with him. He knew she'd never let him spend the night at Haven House. He wasn't about to push his luck, either. She'd stayed an entire night with him, and he had high hopes for countless reoccurrences.

Slipping his arm around Lanier's shoulder, Dallas turned her in the direction of the house. They'd had another beautiful night together, and he was happy to end it on a high note. As the couple reached the front porch, Dallas again brought Lanier into his arms, kissing her with every ounce of passion he was capable of. Making contact with her luscious lips had him feeling wanton.

Dallas wasn't surprised that he desired Lanier, because there was never a time that he didn't. His mind made love to her day and night. She was the last person he thought of at night, and in the morning she was back in his head.

Dallas really didn't want to go. "Good night, babe. Dream of me. I love you more than I did yesterday. By tomorrow, I'll love you even more."

"I always dream of you. Good night, Dallas. I love you more."

Dallas stood at the bottom of the porch steps until Lanier disappeared inside.

As he walked away, he wore a dreamy smile. Things were much better between them. Even though he still had reservations about how long it would last, he was determined to let this new phase continue to play out.

Dallas heard Lanier calling him, and he walked back to the porch. "Is everything okay?"

Lanier shook her head. "I need you. Will you stay longer? I don't want to be alone." There was no way

Dallas could turn down her request. The pleading look in her eyes melted his heart. She had said she needed him, which was another first. He needed her, too, all the time. Rushing up the steps, he lifted her off her feet and carried her inside. As he headed toward the family room, Lanier put her mouth to his ear.

"I want us to go upstairs," she whispered.

He appeared perplexed. "Are you sure?"

"Positive. You can set me down so I can walk."

Dallas took the overstuffed chair while Lanier went through her DVDs, looking for a good movie to watch. It had to be romantic, but not too sexual. He knew where she stood on making love at Haven House. He was the kind of man who respected her rules and wishes, but was she the one in danger of breaking them?

Lanier found a collection of romantic sagas, true stories and dramas she loved. After inserting the DVD into the player, Lanier stretched out at the bottom of the bed.

Dallas had watched her every move. Her strides were quick, sure-footed and sleek, and the light swaying of her hips fascinated him. He could sit and watch her for hours without getting bored. She was a force he loved reckoning with.

As hard as it was to do, Dallas turned his eyes to the television. Lanier lying on the bed conjured up a bevy of romantic visions, the type she would want to avoid. Although he'd love to lie down with her, he wouldn't even hint at it. The best thing for him to do was shut off his mind and pay attention to the movie.

A half hour into the movie, Dallas looked over at Lanier again. The drooping of her eyes signaled to him it was time to go. As he was about to tell her he was leaving, she leveled those pretty brown eyes on him, causing him to lose himself in her gaze.

Lanier patted the spot next to her. "Come lay down with me. You look like you're about to fall asleep. I want you comfortable."

"Are you sure?"

Lanier frowned. "Why do you always ask me that? I know my own mind."

"Guilty as charged. Sorry. I'll work on it."

Dallas walked over to the bed and lay down next to Lanier. He lodged a pillow under his head. Turning on his stomach, he repositioned the pillow to make himself more comfortable.

Lanier wanted Dallas in the worst way. Entering into a mental argument with herself, she wondered if rules should apply when she was home alone. The girls weren't there to come bounding into her room unexpectedly. They were five and a half hours away. The sexy man she loved was right beside her.

Deciding to just wait and see what transpired, Lanier turned her attention back to the movie. The film was wonderful and full of intrigue, but it couldn't compete with the man in her bed. Nothing compared to Dallas Carrington. Even though he had spitting images of himself, Dallas was the only man who did it for her.

Inching closer to Lanier, Dallas laid his arm across her stomach. The mere touch sent shockwaves of desire through him. He wanted to make love to Lanier every second of every day. Tonight was no exception. The best thing for him to do would be to leave. Torturing himself like this wasn't heroic. It was insane.

Dallas turned her head to face him. "I need to go. Lying here with you isn't working for me. You have rules I wouldn't think of crossing, but I have a much bigger, harder problem." He looked down at his bulging manhood. "Do you get my drift?"

Lanier laughed. She didn't have anything visual to show how badly she wanted him, but moisture was already flowing from her.

To do Dallas or not to do Dallas is the million-dollar question.

Smiling wickedly, Lanier reached for Dallas's zipper. "I want you and you want me. So what is there to ponder?"

He felt dizzy from the desire welling up in him like a humid summer day. Instead of answering, he let his lips and tongue do the talking.

Chapter 6

Lanier was busy scoping out her closet for attire to wear to the Carrington family dinner when she heard the door chimes peal. She mentally accused the visitor of bad timing; all she had on was a bathrobe, because she'd just finished showering.

Dallas was picking her up at 6:30, and it was now 4:15. It wasn't a lot of time for a lady to pamper herself, but it was all the time she had. Her entire day had been a whirlwind of activity. She'd also slept in late since Dallas had spent the night.

Rushing from the walk-in closet, Lanier slid her feet into flat slippers and hit the steps recklessly. The doorbell had pealed twice more since the initial ring. Something must be pretty darn important for someone to lay insistent fingers on the bell.

Her mind went straight to the girls. Her body trembled slightly.

Had something happened to one of their girls at summer camp?

Peering through the security screen gave her a real shock. It was Barbara—and Joseph wasn't with her. What did she think she was doing popping in uninvited and unannounced?

Perhaps something has happened to Dad.

Lanier opened the door wide. "Mom, I'm surprised to see you. What brings you here?"

Barbara drew in a shaky breath. "I wanted to see my daughter again. I'd like to sit down and have a heart-to-heart. Is this a bad time for you?"

Lanier frowned. "I have a dinner engagement." She paused to collect her thoughts. "Mom, I've already said that I don't want to dredge up the past. There's nothing back there but darkness and despair. I'd love to chat about things in general. If you don't mind, you can come up to my bedroom while I get dressed."

"No, no, I can come back another time. Seeing your beautiful face will hold me over for now."

Lanier felt guilty. "Mom, don't leave. I'll just cancel my dinner date. You came all the way to Galveston for a reason."

Although you and your sick husband never bothered to meet any of my needs.

Lanier's alter ego had unexpectedly weighed in, and she tried to ignore the bitterness. Dallas suddenly came to mind. Knowing he'd be upset by her absence, she cringed inwardly.

Lanier pulled back to avoid hugging Barbara. The hugs they'd shared at their first meeting had felt awkward for Lanier, especially embracing her father. She'd felt like she were hugging aliens from another planet, yet she'd managed to make the best of a fragile situation.

Lanier had once thought it was impossible to have a relationship with either parent, but she truly wanted to be a part of her natural family. It was a strange feeling, yet it was indeed real. While growing up, she had hoped fervently for her parents to rescue her from the foster homes. Many nights she'd tried convincing herself it was all only a bad dream. Her life with so many dysfunctional families had left her craving a stable family life.

If her parents were clean and sober, she should do all she could to help pull the family back together. Dallas often reminded her that Rome wasn't built in a day and neither was anything else worth having. A lot of nurturing was needed all around.

Making direct eye contact with Barbara wasn't easy for Lanier. Sucking it up, she did it anyway. Barbara and Joseph were still strangers to her.

"Follow me upstairs, Mom. Once I'm dressed, if there's time, I'd love to give you a house tour. We can walk the property another time."

"Lanier," Barbara said sternly, "we need to talk without distractions. I know you say you don't want to talk about our past, but, honey, we have no choice in the matter. This family cannot move forward without settling old scores and moving them out of the way. No matter what you think, your past will put a deadly choke hold on your present and future. This comes from someone who knows firsthand."

The anger inside Lanier was threatening to burst loose, but she was determined to tamp it down.

How dare this woman come into my home and tell me what to do.

Barbara may've had that right when she was a child, but Lanier believed neither of her parents had a say in her adult life.

Trying to find the least painful words to make her mother understand, Lanier fell silent. This situation called for taking a road that offered the least resistance. "At some point we can talk about whatever you need to. We can't do it now. I know I said I'd cancel my plans, but I realized it wouldn't be fair to Dallas. You and I can have lunch again. We can meet here and I'll fix us a nice meal."

Giving in to her daughter's wishes, Barbara followed Lanier up the stairs and into the loft-style bedroom. She sat down on the overstuffed chair. "I like the idea of another lunch date. I hope it's soon." Barbara cleared her throat. "Child, I don't think you realize how much regret I live with from day to day."

"I'm trying to understand," Lanier said, "but it isn't easy."

"Making amends with you will hopefully help me get over a horrific past and give me an opportunity to carve out a brighter future. Your dad is a walking, talking miracle. His liver was damaged beyond repair, or so we were told.

"We found God, and that gave us hope." Looking for a reaction, her eyes locked with Lanier's for several seconds. It was utterly impossible to read her daughter. "Joseph refused to go on the list for a liver donor because he knew he'd created this awful existence for himself. He thought someone who'd made far better choices deserved the transplant. He had consciously destroyed his liver by excessive drinking and the use of street drugs."

Lanier's stomach twisted. To keep her mother from seeing her tears, she excused herself. Finding refuge inside the walk-in closet, her tears rolled free. A few moments later, Lanier pulled two separated pantsuits from a rack. Walking back into the room, she held up both outfits for her mother to see. "What do you think? Which one is best for an informal dinner?"

Lanier remembered a time when her mother had been a fashion plate, wearing nothing but the best attire money could buy. That was a lifetime ago. Even though Barbara was dressed nicely, it didn't compare to how she used to look.

Barbara laughed inwardly, not daring to laugh out loud for fear of Lanier misinterpreting. The ground beneath them was extremely fragile. She didn't want to risk tearing them apart again.

"Honestly, I don't think either one is appropriate, Lanier. They're beautiful but too businesslike, stiff and proper. I get the feeling you didn't even look at what you pulled down. I could tell you'd gotten emotional." She got to her feet. "Let's look at your summer outfits and come up with something fun but daring."

"Great idea! You were right. I got emotional, and I didn't want you to know."

"A mother always knows her child's hurts, even when she's not present."

Barbara went through the closet with Lanier, pushing

clothes back on the rack to separate them. The majority of the hanging attire was more appropriate for dressier occasions. "Where are your shorts and jeans and other summer casuals?"

Lanier pointed at a chest of drawers. "In there. Some things hanging up could work for this dinner, but I haven't put my finger on anything. I guess we should broaden our horizons," Lanier said, walking over to the dresser and opening a drawer near the bottom. "My jeans and shorts are in here. Tops are in the ones below."

A pair of green khaki pants caught Barbara's eye. "What about these?"

Barbara closed the drawer and opened the one beneath it, where she rifled through Lanier's tops. The checkered shirt she came up with had green, brown and beige in it, with slim threads of gold outlining the patches of color.

"These go together perfectly. What do you think?"

"I like it. It'll work."

Lanier suddenly wanted the sham of a bonding session over with, and she would've gone along with anything Barbara had chosen. They were so uncomfortable in each other's presence. Lanier realized a lot of work had to be done before they could become anything special to each other.

Was it even possible for us to act like mother and daughter? Had I felt more comfortable at lunch because Dallas had been at my side? He did have a relaxing effect on me.

"It's time for me to take off so you can finish getting ready," Barbara said, as if she'd read Lanier's mind. It bothered her that her daughter would rather be anywhere but in her presence, yet Barbara knew exactly why it was that way.

Lanier glanced at the clock. It really didn't matter what time it was, because it was simply time for this unplanned meeting to be over. "It *is* getting late. Dallas will be here shortly, and I don't want to keep him waiting."

"Is your relationship with him serious?"

The question irritated Lanier, since it had recently been asked by Casey. It was too personal of a question, and it was nobody's business. "We're happy together, and we're exclusive. Dallas is an extraordinary man."

He's nothing like the poor excuse of a man you hooked up with, Mother.

Lanier mentally berated herself for her dark thoughts. She wasn't surprised at the anger she felt, but she didn't like how awful it made her feel. She'd been angry almost as long as she'd been alive. It was hard to do, but she finally had to admit she wasn't as far along on her path to forgiveness as she'd thought. None of this was easy on her. Lanier was positive it wasn't a walk in the park for her parents, either.

"There is something I really need to say, since you brought up my relationship with Dallas. Because of you and Dad, I've had a hard time getting involved in close relationships. You guys really did a horrific number on me. You left me with a lifetime of nightmares."

Barbara looked sad. "I know. Somehow I convinced myself we weren't affecting you."

"I was only a child. How could you not affect me? I've seen more bad stuff go down between you and Dad than most adults have witnessed. I can still hear the yelling, cursing, name-calling and the violence. I relived it every day of my life. I had zero trust in people and had no desire to fall in love. If what you two portrayed was love, I wanted no part of it. Dallas is the only man who ever understood me and my ever-changing moods, yet it took me forever to trust him."

"I'm glad you and Dallas have each other," Barbara said sincerely. "I wish you the best. But I wonder how he really feels about your checkered background."

I'm not the one responsible for the checkered background, as you so poorly put it. Everything bad that happened to me was because two people who should've loved me didn't.

Lanier swallowed hard to keep from making a bitter retort. "I'll walk you out. Sorry, I have to go." She was actually overjoyed she had somewhere to go. If not, no telling how long this visit might've lasted. Being alone with her mother was pretty scary to her. It made her think of too many violent incidents that she'd spent her entire life trying to forget.

Do I really want to conjure up all that madness again?

Lanier had no choice in the matter if she continued to try to have an amicable relationship with her parents. There was no way for her to let things slide forever, especially when her parents weren't taking responsibility for anything.

At the front door, the two women hugged. It wasn't any less awkward this time, either.

Barbara hesitantly took hold of Lanier's hand. "Please call me about lunch. I'd love us to discuss our feelings. We can't move forward until we do."

With so much anger inside of her, Lanier didn't know how much she could possibly share with them. Her heart was not involved in this relationship. What she really had to do was figure out if she wanted to surrender her heart to people who'd already shattered it into millions of tiny pieces.

"I'll call, Mom. I can't say when. I'm in the process of purchasing a townhome." Biting down on her tongue, Lanier wished she hadn't revealed her personal business.

Barbara looked surprised. "You're moving?"

"It's a long story. I'll tell you about it later. I need to put on my makeup and get dressed," she said, purposely skirting the issue.

The look on Barbara's face let Lanier know she was displeased with her response.

"I'll see you soon, Mom. Have a good evening."

"You do the same," Barbara said, sounding rather chilly. She walked out the door.

Lanier's heart felt heavy with sadness. Knowing she hadn't been as warm as she had been on their first meeting made her feel even worse. Was she hoping for too much, putting too much pressure on herself? Could she really have a decent relationship with the woman who'd brought her into the world, only to abandon her in the days of her greatest need?

Just a short time ago, Lanier had actually believed she could put it all behind her, but she was no longer sure. Was she failing herself again if she couldn't?

Could she really change that much, or *was there too much water under the bridge?*

* * *

The Carrington family and their guests couldn't wait to consume the delicious-smelling food that had their stomachs growling. Until dinner was served, Lanier, Dallas, Ashleigh and Austin hung out in the family room. Little Austin was fast asleep on his mother's lap. Angelica and Beaumont were in the kitchen assisting Houston and Kelly.

As usual, everything one could want was on the menu. Houston and Kelly had decided to put on a Tex-Mex style dinner. Beaumont had wanted to use his beloved grill, so Houston had given in and had allowed him to prepare beef and chicken fajitas.

Lanier loved to just sit and watch the Carrington family interact with one another. Houston had offered to include Lanier's parents in the dinner festivities, but she felt that their presence would cause her undue anxiety. Though she felt a wee bit closer to her mother, the earlier meeting had been overly complicated and had felt horribly unnatural.

Lanier wasn't sure she'd measure up to her parents' idea of success, whatever that was. As far as she knew, they'd never expressed any specific goals for her life. She hadn't been able to tell them about her college degrees and employment as a social worker, which had caused her countless moments of deep sadness. She planned to share the important matters with her mother, but she had no idea when. Simply put, Barbara and Joseph had missed out on a great deal of their daughter's life.

The first communication from her parents had come to Lanier several months ago in the form of an emotional letter penned by her mother. Lanier wished she hadn't started thinking about them. They stole away her joy.

Disliking the sudden brooding look on Lanier's face, Dallas walked over and dropped down next to her on the sofa. His eyes connected with hers. He had watched her earlier, greeting his family members and other guests with a cheerful attitude, but now she had isolated herself and had gone into deep thought. She had done a complete change on him yet again. If only he could figure her out.

Lanier was as complicated as geometry was for a first grader. She had been quiet from the time he'd picked her up at Haven House, and during the drive she'd only spoken in response to his questions, contributing nothing to the conversation on her own.

Dallas was worried about her, yet fussing over her would only make matters worse. If he tried to coddle her, she'd go deeper into her protective shell. He should be used to her quick change in moods by now, but he wasn't. Dallas loved her happier, more carefree moods, which he'd experienced a lot over the past six weeks.

The Lanier of past weeks had been bubbly and full of life, acting as if she were ready to shower the world with glee. This evening's Lanier had turned moody, dark and distant. The icy chill he'd felt in the vehicle had come directly from her. Instead of stealing covert glances at her every couple of minutes, he'd made it a point to keep his eyes on the road. Otherwise, he knew he would confront her about it, which would only serve to make matters worse.

"Want to take a walk? Mom says it'll be an hour or so before dinner is on the table. We have plenty of time to stroll down to the nearest lake."

"Sounds like a good idea. The aromas coming out of the kitchen are making me hungrier by the second." Forcing a smile to her lips, Lanier took Dallas's hand, and her present mood didn't keep her from thoroughly enjoying the magic in his touch.

The couple stepped off the porch. Unable to stop smiling, Dallas tossed his arm around Lanier's slim waist. "You feel good. I love looking at, touching and tasting you." Dallas chuckled. "If we were alone, I'd invite you to skinny-dip with me. You're beautiful in and out of clothes."

As Dallas thought about Lanier and him naked in the lake, his heart thundered and his cheeks glowed with warmth. His hard sex had him wanting to slip away with Lanier and glide his way inside her. Dallas knew he'd go to any lengths to try to cheer her up. "If we were swimming in the lake, out of the way of prying eyes, would you give yourself to me?"

"Of course," she said huskily. "But I don't know how much swimming would take place."

Conjuring up a vivid picture of him and her making love in the water, Lanier wished they were alone at his place, where they could use the pool and the Jacuzzi. But they weren't, she quietly told herself. Chuckling inwardly, Lanier thought of how quickly her bad-girl persona had responded to his challenge. It had also cheered her up.

Coming upon a grassy knoll, Dallas dropped down

onto the thick patch of green, pulling Lanier down to nestle on his lap. She felt the hardness of his manhood through his shorts. Turning him on was a pleasant feeling, though it wasn't something they could do much about at the moment.

Desperate to shake her dark mood, Lanier covered Dallas's mouth with hers, kissing him passionately. Teasing him with her tongue made her hot with physical yearning. "I want you."

Dallas sighed. Lanier's mood was changing for the better, and he fervently returned her kisses.

His fingers stroked her face. "Think you can hold your desire in check until later?"

Laughing, Lanier shook her head. "I can barely wait another minute." Even though there was nowhere on the property for them to go and make love, she was happy he physically desired her. Thoughts of Dallas making love to her helped ward off her dark moods.

Lanier was dressed in all white in a tunic top and jeans that hugged her bombshell frame. On her feet she wore white sandals.

Dallas threaded his hand through her long hair. "I like what you're wearing. Those jeans are getting a real workout on your body."

Lanier didn't tell him she'd put on an outfit her mother had chosen for her and then had taken it off. If she started talking about her mother, there was no doubt in her mind that a foul mood would return.

Not sure if his eyes had focused properly, he took a closer look at her tresses. "When'd you get your hair colored?"

Lanier was elated he'd noticed the change. "Couple

hours after you left this morning, I went into the salon. Like the highlights?"

"Yeah, they complement your mahogany complexion. I love it. Why did you only do streaks?"

"Highlights," she scolded softly. "I didn't want to completely change the color of my hair. I thought about getting it a bit lighter than this, but I chickened out. This is the color I was left with."

"It's beautiful. I can imagine how you might've felt if I hadn't noticed at all. It really glows when the sun hits it." Dallas ran his hand through his hair and shook his head. "Maybe I should color mine," he said, laughing.

Lanier laughed, too. His laughter was as contagious as his charming smile. "I'm thrilled you noticed. You're good at paying attention to me."

Lanier had already checked out Dallas from head to toe. He looked so handsome dressed in black denim jeans and a black Western-style shirt. He loved Texas as much as anyone but didn't routinely wear Western gear. He had gorgeous Stetsons in several colors but only wore them for special events. Most Texans wouldn't be caught dead without hats. During the city of Houston's yearly rodeo and livestock show, Dallas usually dressed the part of a proud Texan. He'd taken Lanier to a rodeo and its concerts two years running.

"We probably should go back inside. We don't want them to eat without us."

"We haven't been gone long, Lanier. Are you hungry?"

"Now I am. I'm not sure I would've eaten much if I was still in a bad mood. I know you noticed. I'm sorry I put you through it."

Dallas got to his feet then helped Lanier up. Bringing her into his arms, he kissed her passionately. "I don't like your dark moods, and I don't always understand, but I'm here to help you find your way out of them."

Lanier wrapped her leg up around Dallas's thigh. "Thank you for being here. Seeing my mother earlier upset me. The visit just didn't go well."

Dallas raised both eyebrows. "Your mother came to the house? Did you know she was coming?"

"She came…and no, I didn't know about it. I was stunned."

Dallas didn't know what to say but felt he had to say something. "Listen, you can't allow people to control you. If you didn't want to see your mom, you should've told her. Take some responsibility for yourself, Lanier. Instead of saying it was bad timing, you punished yourself. She was insensitive by showing up without calling. When will you get it?"

Lanier heard the anger and frustration in his voice and it stung. He was right, though. "I thought I had it. I know I have to do better."

"Yes, you do, much better! People walk over you 'cause you allow it. Every time someone upsets you it affects our relationship. I'm tired of seeing you in a bad mood that someone else is responsible for. You *have* to control your moods—not others."

Lanier couldn't argue with the truth. She was sorry that she'd caused yet another tiff in their relationship, and she hoped it wouldn't ruin the rest of the evening.

"Come here, you." He brought her head to his chest. "I shouldn't have come down on you so hard. Sorry for the anger. Until you understand that you're leaving your happiness up to perfect strangers, biological or not, you'll remain unhappy. Live the life you want, and stop dwelling in the misery that life's circumstances has forced upon you."

Lanier lifted her head and frowned. "It sounds so simple when you say it. Why can't I move on? Why can't I forget?" She shrugged.

"Only you can answer those questions, Lanier. You owe yourself that much."

Wiping away an errant tear, Lanier nodded. "I'm the only person I owe something to, but that's not how I live. I feel like I owe the entire world because my parents abandoned me and other people had to take care of me, even those who did a lousy job of it."

"Is that why you got into the foster care business?"

"I'm sure it had something to do with it in the beginning. I wanted to give back and do much better by the kids living at Haven House. The girls have brought so much joy. I can hardly wait to help out other kids in need."

"You're good at what you do, and you don't do it because you feel you owe somebody. It's what you dreamed of doing as a foster child. If you never take in another needy child, you'll still be the same person I've come to know and love. Give yourself a break."

"So, are you saying highlights don't help the changes I'm trying to make?"

Dallas laughed. The look on Lanier's face was so pitifully cute and innocent. All he wanted was to brighten her mood and hear her laugh. Picking her up, he swung her around. "Lighten up, will you? You are still the same beautiful you."

Lanier had thought the highlights might make her appear bolder and more daring. Instead of trying to explain it, she laughed at herself.

Dallas felt rewarded by her laughter. "Let's go eat. I'm ready to stuff my face."

"I could do some serious damage myself. Did you see those homemade tamales Kelly had her Mama Tillie make?"

"Mom ran me out the kitchen right after I peeked into a pot of refried beans. I've got to be supercareful. I can't afford to gain an ounce of weight before our season ends."

Lanier scanned his body, loving all of what she saw. "You're perfect, Dallas, just the way you are. I'll put you in check if you run into trouble."

"Thanks. I might need your help," he joked.

As soon as the family was seated, large platters of meat and huge bowls of vegetables were passed around. They had a Tex-Mex feast of grilled beef brisket, tri-tip steak, chicken and beef fajitas, cheese enchiladas, red beans, refried beans and homemade tortillas. Several types of salads were served, and the favorite was a spicy taco salad.

Lanier thought about all the times she'd been at a Carrington table. She loved how they came together to make family dinners happen. Houston was this evening's host, but all family members and guests had contributed to the feast in one way or another.

With Dallas seated right next to her, Lanier had the urge to reach under the table and squeeze his thigh. Another man would've left her a long time ago, but he did his best to understand her past trials and deal with the things she still put herself through. Dallas was the right man for her.

Am I the right woman for him?

It was a question she asked herself often but could never answer honestly. Dallas deserved no less than the very best woman as a lifelong mate. Ashleigh and Austin were an ideal couple, and Houston and Kelly followed in their footsteps. The parents' marriage was a model one. The Carringtons were a loving family, but she wasn't sure if her troubled background had a place among them.

Dallas dipped up a spoonful of red beans and held it to Lanier's mouth. "Try these. You'll be missing out on something delicious if you don't." Dallas knew Lanier wasn't a big fan of beans because she'd been fed them on a regular basis in foster homes. She'd sworn off beans once she was out on her own.

To keep from drawing any attention, Lanier accepted the food. She tried to swallow the beans without tasting them, but she couldn't get it all down at once. Then she nodded, raising her eyebrows. "Maybe I need to rethink my aversion. These *are* delicious."

Austin stood and asked for everyone's attention. "I won't keep you from your plates too long." He reached for Ashleigh's hand. "We've got good news to share. My golden girl and I are pregnant again. In about seven months, we'll have a brand-new Carrington. We're making sure this one isn't born on a cruise ship. It was kind of exciting, but we're sticking close to home."

Congratulations came loudly from all around the table.

Ashleigh already had the special glow most pregnant

women sported. She got to her feet and planted a passionate kiss onto her husband's mouth. "Kelly, we won't mind if you're around to help deliver the newcomer. In fact, we'd be honored. We're leaning toward having the baby at the ranch with a midwife. We'll keep everyone informed." Smiling broadly, Ashleigh reclaimed her chair.

"That's it, family. Continue eating, drinking and be merry," Austin enthused.

Dallas clapped and the others followed suit.

Lanier was so happy for Ashleigh, but she was disappointed that she hadn't moved on like her best friend had.

Would I ever announce a pregnancy? More important, would I ever be Dallas's wife?

Lanier loved him so much, but she had to be further along in changing her outlook on life to be the best person for him. Dallas deserved a happy wife, not a burdensome one. At that very moment she thought of her mother and father. Lanier couldn't imagine Barbara holding a baby, and she wasn't sure she'd ever trust Joseph to cradle any child belonging to her. She closed her eyes and tried to stop the negative chatter inside her head.

Kelly walked up to Dallas and briefly took his hand. "You were brilliant in the last game. Houston nearly lost his mind when you hit that last home run. Keep up the good work. I'm proud of you, D."

Grinning, Dallas bent his head and kissed Kelly's cheek. "Thanks. It looks like we have a shot at the big showdown."

"It's more than a shot, D. People have already put money on the Hurricanes."

Dallas nodded. "Thanks for the encouragement. Will you make it to more games?"

"Whenever it's possible. Thanks for including me."

Dallas smiled. "You're my future sister-in-law. By the way, have you two set a wedding date?" Dallas hated sneaking in that question, but if he could end Houston's misery, it'd be well worth it.

Kelly shuffled her feet. "Not yet. I'm trying to give Houston plenty of time to get used to the idea of being married. I'd marry him today if I was sure he was ready. When we walk down the aisle, I want it to be forever for us."

Dallas smiled again. "You really are someone special. Having you looking out for him means a great deal to Houston, but he can hardly wait to take the walk of his lifetime. Houston *is* ready to marry you. You can take that to the bank."

Kelly looked pleasantly surprised. "You said that with such strong conviction. Has he told you something he hasn't shared with me?"

"I just know what I know. Houston is ready. Trust me."

Houston would kill Dallas if he thought he had been pressuring Kelly. If his brother took issue with his technique, he could explain himself.

"Everyone, please get together for a minute," Angelica requested. "Dad and I brought a video of the boys when they were younger. Who wants to see it?"

"I do," Kelly shouted.

"Me, too," Ashleigh chimed in, even though she'd already seen it umpteen times.

"Guys, is it okay?" Angelica asked her sons.

"It's fine, Mom. Set up the video in the family room whenever you're ready. We can eat dessert while watching," Houston responded.

Angelica loved showing tapes of her boys in action, and no one would've turned down her request. Angelica had been the top team mom in every sport they'd played, and Beaumont had usually volunteered to assist coaches or had taken on a job as one.

"Come into the family room when you're ready," Beaumont said. "We'll be waiting."

Chapter 7

While driving Lanier home, Dallas kept his eyes on the road. She was still in a good mood, but he wasn't. Seeing so much love pouring from the television screen in Houston's home had brought back so many incredible memories. That Lanier had been denied the same kind of love bothered him. She had been treated like garbage by people she had trusted. What had happened to her might ruin her chances of ever finding real happiness. That was more painful than anything he could think of. If she couldn't find happiness with herself, she'd never find it with him.

Lanier reached over and put her hand on Dallas's thigh. "Are you tired of me?"

"No," he readily responded. "What makes you think that?"

"I just wanted to know. Since you're not, is it okay if I go to your place for a while? I'm not sleepy yet."

A huge grin swept across Dallas's lips. "I'd love to take you home with me. I'm surprised you asked. Don't you want to be alone?"

"I don't want to be without you. I was sulky a good bit of the evening, and I want to make it up to you."

"Lanier, you don't have to do any such thing. I know what you're going through. After you told me your mother had dropped in on you, I understood your mood."

"Okay, I won't try to make up for anything. But I still want to go home with you."

"I want that as much as you do. We're on our way." He made a quick U-turn to head back in the direction of his home.

Cranberry-scented votive candles burned brightly in crystal holders on the coffee table in the spacious family room. The recessed lighting was dimmed to its lowest capacity, and the electric fireplace was glowing. The white window shutters in the family room were thrown open, providing a panoramic view of the largest lake on the property. Autumn was Dallas's favorite season, and he loved cooler temperatures.

Dressed only in one of Dallas's white silk shirts and a pair of his athletic socks, Lanier was comfortable and fully relaxed seated on the sofa beside Dallas. She smoothed his waves with the palm of her hand and looked into his warm eyes. Lately, she often found herself wondering what he was thinking.

Over the past month, Dallas appeared to be deep in thought more frequently. It could be baseball playoffs or it could be something more personal and private. There was so much unsaid between them. She blamed herself for the unspoken words that desperately needed to be voiced. While she knew what she'd like to say to him, she fell short on courage.

Lazing his forefinger down the side of her face, his eyes connected with hers. He wanted to tell her more often how much he loved her, but he didn't want to scare her, so he tried to control his feelings.

"Are you warm enough, sweetheart? If not, I can turn down the air conditioner."

A lazy smile formed on her lips. "Hot is more like it. I always feel overheated when I'm with you. I know you get sick of hearing that." She placed her finger on his thigh and made a sizzling hiss to show him the effect touching him had on her. "Does that answer your question?"

"It does." Leaning over, Dallas drew her lower lip into his mouth, sucking on it gently. "Touching you produces the same kind of heat in me." He brought her onto his lap. Nuzzling his nose against her neck, he inhaled the perfumed scent of her skin. "I never get sick of anything about you." His grin was full of mischief. "I know what I have on under my pajama bottoms, but I'm not sure what you're hiding or not hiding. Want to clue me in?"

Lanier laughed gently. "No, but I won't keep you from exploring on your own to find out." Knowing she had nothing on under her shirt, she laughed inwardly. The shirt was long, but if she felt his nudity beneath his pajamas, he should be able to feel hers.

Instead of putting his hand under the shirt, Dallas began exploring her body through the soft material.

At first touch, his manhood snapped to attention. As he had suspected, she wore nothing beneath the top. Slowly, tantalizingly, he stroked her smooth-as-silk bare legs. Gently clamping his mouth down over hers, he kissed her deeply, tasting and teasing her mouth with his tongue. He moaned with yearning.

As far as Dallas was concerned, Lanier was as sexy as women came, but she had an aura of innocence that had remained untouched. Thinking about the first time he'd made love to her always drove him a bit crazy. It was a night he'd never forget. She'd cried afterward, worried that he'd thought she'd been an easy conquest. Nothing could've been further from the truth. They had dated at least six months before giving in to one another.

They could've made love on the first night of meeting and Dallas would've still thought Lanier was a treasure. She had been a virgin. She had dated but had never found anyone who understood her. One previous relationship that had had potential hadn't worked because the man she was involved with had been too immature to respect decisions she'd made for her life. Had she not fallen in love with him, Dallas was sure she would've ended it with him, too.

Lanier flashed her eyes at him. "Are you up for being seduced?"

Dallas opened his arms wide in a gesture of surrender. "Seduce me."

Sliding her hand up under his pajama top, Lanier stroked Dallas's broad chest. While rolling his nipple between her thumb and forefinger, she loved his jerking reaction to the sensations running through him. Her gentle giant was extremely sensuous and very sensitive.

He never failed to let her know how much he ached for her.

Dallas rolled Lanier on top of his outstretched body. His hands slipped under the back of the shirt but went no farther than the top of her thighs. While massaging her flesh with his fingertips, it was hard to keep his hands off her sweet, firmly rounded buttocks. He had no intentions of denying himself the pleasure much longer.

It was hard for Lanier to keep from squirming. Dallas's manhood was granite-hard, and she couldn't help thinking of how wonderful it felt when he was inside her. The man knew how to satisfy her and held nothing back. She was glad he didn't make her beg; dignity was a hard thing to muster up when she wanted him this badly. She couldn't even count the times she'd awakened in the middle of the night desiring him like crazy, wanting to call him to come be with her. With young girls in the house, that wasn't a luxury she had been privy to.

Looking up at her, he studied her stunning features. Desire was in her eyes, and he was sure his own eyes mirrored the same. "Let's go into the bedroom."

"Let's not." Looking over at the fireplace, she pointed at the plush white rug laid out in front of it. "I want you to take me there."

Dallas's heart took off to the races. "That I can deliver."

Taking her by the hand, he led her over to the fireplace. Dallas lay down and guided her on top of him. He cupped her face in both his hands and kissed her thoroughly. It was now time to get down to serious business. Fully satisfying his beautiful woman was the only thing on his mind.

His hands once again snaked up under her shirt. This time his fingers went straight for her firm behind, squeezing it gently. Rolling her off him, he laid her on her back and hovered over her, kissing her until they both were breathless.

Dallas's hands stroked her intimate core, his fingers probing inside where her flesh was soft, warm and wet. Knowing how much she liked foreplay, he did to her body all the things that drove her insane. His head began a slow descent to the lower part of her body and his mouth and tongue followed the same moisture-laden path his fingers had taken.

"Dallas, I'm ready, ready for you to take me there. Please…" She moaned softly.

"Hold on to me, baby. I'm as ready as you are. I love you, Lanier."

Pushing up her shirt, he exposed her nakedness, his eyes roving over her body for an instant. Poised slightly above her, he lowered his body just enough to gain him entry. Heavy gasps escaped his lips as he slowly made his way inside her, where their body heat mingled, inducing a firestorm within.

Time and time again, he plunged in and out of her, stroking slowly and tenderly. Dallas continuously filled her up with his hardened flesh. Lanier matched his exquisite strokes, rising up to meet each one, drawing him as deep into her as he could go.

Clinging to Dallas as if he were a lifeline, Lanier felt her body shaking, rattling and rolling. As her climax came upon on her with uncontrollable force, tears of passion streamed from her eyes. "Yes," she cried out, "yes."

Every time Dallas made love to Lanier it was different, but it was always spectacularly physical and highly charged with emotions. Feeling his body shuddering hard then slowly going numb, he buried his face against her shoulder, tremendously enjoying the powerful release. He'd never admit it to her, but making love to her wore him out completely.

Dallas awakened and found that Lanier had already gotten up. He knew she hadn't left because he'd driven her there. Getting up from the floor, he stumbled languidly toward the back of the house. As he entered the master bedroom, he heard water running in the adjoining bathroom. A peek inside the room revealed a naked Lanier standing under cascading water inside the glass-enclosed shower. He stood there and stared at her for several seconds, mesmerized by her beauty.

Dallas entered the bathroom, opened the shower door and stepped inside.

Lanier turned, smiling brightly at him. "I wanted to wake you before I came in here, but you looked so peaceful." She wound her arms around his neck. "I'm glad you came looking for me."

Lanier adjusted the water temperature to Dallas's preference. Like her, he was into steamy hot water with lots of bubbles and oils. Picking up a tube of wild cherry blossom shower gel and a bath sponge, Lanier scrubbed his body, standing on tiptoes to reach his shoulders.

Drenching the sponge with water, Lanier drizzled out the sudsy liquid all over his body. As she moved down to his genitals, she couldn't help smiling broadly at how well-endowed Dallas was, even when not aroused.

After Lanier rinsed off Dallas, she grabbed a bottle of shampoo. He loved it when she washed his hair, and she jumped right into it, lathering up his waves and scrubbing his scalp vigorously.

After stepping out of the shower, Dallas and Lanier took turns drying off each other's bodies. Large bath sheets easily extracted the moisture from their water-soaked skin. As they took turns applying lotion to their limbs, they felt totally relaxed. Lanier knew she could fall back to sleep at the drop of a hat, but that'd have to wait.

After slipping into his bathrobe, Dallas playfully tousled her hair, which now hung completely straight from the moisture. "Are you hungry?"

"After that vigorous romp on the carpet, I'm starving. What do you have in mind?" She slipped on a white bathrobe Dallas held open for her.

He looked at a clock on the black-and-gold granite dressing table. "It's too late to have anything delivered in. Let's just go raid the refrigerator. I bought groceries recently, so we'll have lots of goodies to choose from."

Lanier chuckled. "I'm all for goodies." Walking up to Dallas, she stood on tiptoes and kissed him passionately. "I'm eager to see what you shopped for. At 3:00 a.m., it's closer to breakfast time than anything else, but I'm not in the mood for that."

Dallas's humongous futuristic kitchen had a wrap-around breakfast bar and endless cherrywood cabinets, burnished granite counters and stainless-steel appliances. The flooring was made of beautiful earth-tone slate tiles, complemented by a matching backsplash.

Lanier always had a good laugh when she opened the built-in refrigerator, the largest one she'd ever seen.

Lanier turned around to say something to Dallas, but he was nowhere in sight. Although he had given her permission to get anything she wanted, she still preferred them to pick out something together.

In the refrigerator Lanier spotted several packets of deli-cut luncheon meats wrapped in white paper. Dallas loved to make huge sandwiches drowned in mayonnaise and mustard.

Pulling a couple of packages from the bin, she read the labels: smoked turkey and salami. She put back everything but the smoked turkey and took out a loaf of whole-wheat bread, which she used to make sandwiches. She made Dallas a triple-decker sandwich, which was how he liked it.

Carrying a sweet-potato pie in his hand, Dallas came in from the garage. "See what I got. Mom held it back for me. Since you fixed three pies, she thought I should take one home."

"Your mom has your back." Lanier cracked up. "I'm glad she saved you one so I can help you eat it. Your sandwich is ready. Where do you want to eat?"

"At the breakfast bar. I don't see any chips or pretzels. I'll get them. Go ahead and sit down," Dallas instructed.

"I know how you love your salty snacks. Sorry I forgot to put out some."

"No big deal. You took care of the main course. I can't wait to bite into that sandwich."

"Triple-decker, just how you like it. I can't deal with

all that bread. Three slices in one sitting is calorie hell for me."

Dallas laughed. "Do you see how big I am? The way I work out, that little bit of bread doesn't stand a chance of becoming a problem for me. What do you want to drink?"

Lanier wanted hot tea, but she didn't want to keep Dallas from eating his sandwich. If she said what she wanted, he'd fix it. "Do you have any Diet Coke with lime?"

"I keep your favorite drink on hand. I'll get you one. I know you want ice."

"Please."

In less than a minute Dallas came back to the breakfast bar with a bag of chips and a Coke and ice for Lanier. He set the items on the counter and mounted a bar stool with ease.

Lanier bit into her sandwich. The meat tasted as fresh as the lettuce and tomatoes. She wasn't a regular sandwich eater, but this one was delicious. "Where'd you get your meat?"

"Harden's Deli. Dad buys special cuts of beef from a butcher friend he's patronized since we were kids. Dad has Mr. Harden divide a whole cow and give each of us equal portions. When my brothers and I see that we have a lot left from the previous purchase, we tell Dad to exclude us until next time."

"He pays for it, too?"

"If we'd let him. We love his generosity, but he taught us that men handle their own business. He can't argue with his own teachings."

"I guess not. It must be nice to have lots of money at

your disposal. I often wonder what it'd be like to shop and not look at prices."

Dallas chuckled. "Little darling, it's not like that with us. Our parents don't buy anything that's not on sale. You should see Mom pouring over grocery ads. She goes to several stores before she's through with her weekly shopping. Angelica Carrington is what we call a professional shopper. She gets a bang from every buck."

Lanier laughed. "I know she shops for clothing that way. I've been to the mall with her."

Dallas nodded. "If it's not on sale, she's not buying it. That's how rich people stay wealthy."

If you were my wife, you could have anything your heart desired. Price wouldn't even enter into it. All you'd have to do is pick out what you want and take it to the register. I'd buy you the world if it was up for sale.

The couple grew silent, concentrating on eating and drinking.

As Dallas thought back on the evening, he was pleased more by the latter part than its onset. Learning that Austin and Ashleigh were pregnant again had made him happy, but it had also made him long for a family of his own. Dallas didn't want to be an old father. Like his father, he wanted to be involved in every aspect of his kids' lives. If he had sons, he hoped they'd be interested in playing sports, but he'd love them no less if they chose to play the piano, sing in the choir or enter into some other profession of their own choosing. He'd feel the same way about daughters.

Lanier nudged Dallas with her shoulder. "Where are you? I feel like I'm here alone."

Leaning over, Dallas kissed her on the chin. "I'm here, babe. Just got caught up in thinking about the dinner at Houston's. Sorry if I made you feel left out."

Happy for his attention, she laid her head on his shoulder. "Want anything else to eat?"

"I'm good. What about you?"

"Couldn't eat another bite. Once I clean up in here, I'd like to go to bed."

"Okay. I'll get dressed and take you home. Leave the kitchen. I'll get it when I come back from your place."

Lanier suddenly looked disheartened. "I didn't say I wanted to go home. I want to go to sleep in your bed. If that's not what you want, I'll get dressed."

"Sweetheart, you know I want you here with me. When will you get it through your thick skull that I love wrapping you up in my arms? I can't believe that after all this time you can't say to me exactly what you mean. It's frustrating when I have to try and second-guess you."

"I don't see it that way."

"You never do. It's kind of insulting when you make negative assumptions about me. I don't know what you want or need if you don't tell me. I'm also left to assume. When you said you wanted to go to bed, I assumed you meant your bed. Had you said I'm ready to get into your bed, I wouldn't have had to assume. It's not that difficult to make yourself clear."

Lanier didn't want to argue. Without commenting, she got down off the stool and took her plate and glass over to the sink, where she rinsed everything off and stacked it all in the dishwasher. She then went back for Dallas's plate and glass, repeating the same steps.

Coming up behind Dallas, she wound her arms around him, kissing his neck. "One day I'm going to stop assuming that you don't want me around. You let me know that you want me in so many ways, but my uncertainty continues. I'm going to get into your bed."

She felt Dallas's eyes intently on her as she left the kitchen. She had managed to frustrate him yet again. Getting into bed and falling asleep was on her mind. She didn't want to go home. He wanted her to stay, and she desired to sleep in his arms.

Lanier went into the bathroom and brushed her teeth with a toothbrush Dallas had given her the first night she'd stayed there. After running warm water over a facecloth, she wiped off her face and hands.

"Bedtime," she said to herself. "I'm going to sleep like I've been deprived for weeks."

Dallas hadn't come back to the room yet, so she took off the robe and got in bed. After she turned off the bedside lamp, she pulled the comforter up over her nude body.

Dallas entered the master bedroom and went straight through to the bathroom. Because Lanier's eyes were closed, he thought she was asleep. At the same time, he hoped she wasn't. He hadn't gotten his good-night kiss. In fact, he wouldn't mind receiving a few more kisses from the lady with the sweetest lips.

Dallas came out of the bathroom and came to a stop when he was a few steps from his bed. His eyes devoured Lanier's form. Spotting the robe draped over a chair, he smiled, knowing she had had nothing on beneath it. He loved everything about Lanier, except her bad moods.

His hope for her was total freedom from a past that still had her bound. The new Lanier she'd been revealing to him was intriguing and happy-go-lucky. The highlights in her hair had told him how much she was ready to breathe life into a new image of herself.

To tell the truth, he loved Lanier no matter what. To only love certain parts of a person wasn't true love. Dallas didn't want her to make changes for him; he wanted Lanier happy and in love with herself. Communication was everything, and she had to find a way to do it effectively.

Deciding to let her sleep, Dallas shed his robe and climbed in between the sheets. "I love you," he whispered. "Sleep peacefully."

Lanier was a light sleeper. Dallas getting into bed aroused her, yet she continued to lie perfectly still. Then she slowly scooted across the bed. Without uttering a word, she laid her head on Dallas's chest and covered his heart with her hand.

Lowering his head slightly, he leaned it against hers and closed his eyes. This was what he wanted every night for the rest of his life, but their professions wouldn't allow it to happen until he retired. Plans began to form in his head as he lay there, mentally designing their future.

The peace Lanier experienced lying in Dallas's arms was perfect. Neither of them had to speak a word for everything between them to feel okay. She didn't have to wonder if he was quiet because she'd said or done something wrong. This sweet man could lift Lanier up just being near her. She desperately wanted to be worthy of a man as wonderful as he. She loved that he didn't want her to change anything about herself for him.

Until he'd come into her life, men wanting her to be who she was had been nonexistent. She wanted to do something extremely special for him. Buying him presents wasn't something she'd consider. Lanier wanted to give him something he didn't have or couldn't run out and buy. The only thing he really wanted was for her to find true happiness. It was a tall order, but she was on her way.

How can I prove to him that any changes in me are permanent? That might be impossible when I'm not perfectly sure myself. How can I manage to keep from reverting to my old self? How do I become everything Dallas wants in a woman, the kind of woman he'd love enough to take as his wife? Am I that woman?

Lanier had often asked herself the same questions. Dallas loved her and he didn't have a problem showing it. He loved her enough to make her his wife, because he'd talked to her about marriage before he'd proposed. The problem was that he'd brought it up at times when she wouldn't think of marrying.

Please help me to be ready to be his wife if he asks to marry me again. Mrs. Dallas Carrington is the name I want for the rest of my life. With him, I don't have to compromise who Lanier Watson is.

Just like Dallas, Lanier fell asleep pondering their future.

Bright sunlight shining into the room woke Lanier and she sat up in bed. Nearly blinded by the glowing rays, she rubbed her eyes. Dallas was already up. She was glad she'd slept so well, but she hadn't intended on sleeping this late. It was a few minutes after ten. She'd admit to lying in bed a bit longer now that the girls were away, but never this late.

Slowly, Lanier slipped out of bed. As she looked up, she saw the red vase of fresh flowers on the nightstand. She removed a small card planted among the bright blooms.

> *Good morning, Sunshine. If you wake up and I'm not there, I'll be right back. I'm picking up shirts at the cleaners. Stay in bed as long as you want. My mattress loves your beautiful body, and I love having it entwined with mine.*
> *Love, Dallas*

Chapter 8

The next day, Lanier zipped from her bathroom, where she'd just showered. While grabbing the receiver, she nearly dropped it. "Hello."

"Good morning, Lanier. It's Casey. Sorry we haven't talked in a while. I've got great news—your loan is approved. There are lots of papers to fill out. Please bring in the cashier's check we discussed to open escrow. Can you stop by today?"

Lanier's heart was beating way too fast from the excitement. Dropping down on the bed, she laid her head against a pillow. "I can meet today." She glanced at the clock. It was early.

"How about ten o'clock?"

"Perfect. I'll see you then. The paperwork will be in order. Where is it best to reach you?"

"I'll be home until nine-thirty. Thanks, Casey." Lanier's demeanor was kind of cool.

"You're welcome, Lanier."

Lanier hung up the phone. She buried her face into the pillow and tears flowed. Her feelings weren't all joyous. She also felt fear over what she was undertaking. Ashleigh wasn't in on this real estate deal. Once the paperwork was signed, the town house was her sole responsibility. *I'm a loner in this.* "Don't start second-guessing yourself. You've cleared higher hurdles than this," she told herself.

The personal questions Casey had asked about her and Dallas had come to Lanier's mind during the phone conversation. It was a sticky situation, and she didn't want it to get any stickier.

Do I want to purchase a town house from someone who pried into the private affairs of others, especially from the same someone who worked for the complex where I would reside? Lanier also suspected that the woman had designs on the man she loved.

Lanier's next thought was to call Dallas. Then she decided against it, wanting to wait to tell him in person. If she phoned him, she wouldn't be able to hold back the news. He'd be happy for her. Everything he'd ever told her was for her own good. Seeing her fail at anything would sadden Dallas. The man was in her corner, and he worked hard to get her to be confident in herself. That had been his message to her during the family dinner at Houston's ten days ago.

The phone rang, crashing into her thoughts. Rolling over, she picked it up. "Morning."

"Lanier, this is Patricia Wright, Department of Social Services. I'd like to stop by and see you and Ashleigh. Is today a possibility?"

Lanier looked worried. "Ashleigh isn't in yet. It's still early."

"Okay. I'd just like to talk to both of you about emergency placements, since you're considering putting Haven House on our temporary listing. I want to go over important details."

"As soon as Ash gets here, I'll call you back."

"That's fine with me. I look forward to hearing back from you. Have a great morning."

"You, too, Ms. Wright. You'll hear from us."

The ten o'clock appointment with Casey came to mind. As she wondered if she should call her and cancel, she heard door chimes. *Ashleigh is here.* Maybe she wouldn't have to cancel after all.

Lanier made a mad dash for the staircase. They'd talked about emergency placement before but had yet to make a final decision.

Lanier headed for the office. Spotting Ashleigh in the kitchen making coffee, she popped into the room. "Morning!"

Ashleigh smiled. "Same to you. I'm surprised you're not dressed yet."

Lanier laughed. "I've been kind of a slacker ever since our girls went off to camp." Both women laughed.

Lanier took a seat at the table. "I just got a call from Patricia Wright at Social Services." She shared with Ashleigh what had been said.

Ashleigh appeared thoughtful. "Even though emergency placements are rarely for more than a couple of days, I think we need to get renovations done before we list Haven House. We need to operate without being cramped for space. And we still plan to take in teenage girls eventually, so there has to be enough room for emergency placements."

"I agree," Lanier said.

"We need to start renovations sooner rather than later. Plenty of funds are socked away."

"I have something to tell you, Ash." Lanier shared her good news.

Ashleigh gave Lanier a warm hug. "Congratulations! Have you told Dallas yet?"

"I want to see his reaction. I have an appointment with Casey at ten." Lanier frowned. "I scheduled it before talking to Patricia."

Ashleigh shrugged. "I'll be here all day. We can see her later this afternoon. Sometimes you forget we're in this together. Just because I don't live here anymore doesn't mean I'm not directly involved, 'cause I am. Don't ever feel like I'm not at your disposal. Haven House is *our* baby. We'll continue raising it together."

Lanier looked relieved. "Thanks, Ash. I feel better. I've entertained the idea of canceling my appointment at the complex for personal reasons. Casey has rubbed me the wrong way, and I don't know if I want to live at a place where she works."

"I can understand that. She shouldn't have asked about your personal relationship with Dallas. It is none of her business. You put her in her place, and I'm glad you stood up to her."

Lanier nodded. "I'm proud of how I handled it. It was actually easy."

"If you decide to keep the appointment, do you want a cup of coffee before you leave? I can bring it upstairs."

"I'll throw my clothes on first and come back and drink a cup with you."

"I'd love the company. Want a slice or two of toast?"

"One slice is fine to help absorb the coffee." Lanier blew Ashleigh a kiss. "Be back in a few." Lanier left the kitchen and quickly headed for the steps.

Dallas came back to Lanier's mind as she entered the bedroom. She really wanted to hear his voice. Seeing his reaction to the news was more to her liking. She didn't know if she was taking the town house or not, so it was best not to say anything yet.

Lanier slid down over her head a bright yellow silk top. She slipped on navy blue slacks, and then neatly tucked her top into the waistband. Stepping into the bathroom, she put on her makeup and styled her hair.

Satisfied with how she looked, Lanier returned to the bedroom and retrieved a navy blazer and then looped it through the straps on her navy Coach bag.

Lanier came back into the kitchen and Ashleigh went over to the counter and poured her a cup of hot coffee. Buttered toast had been placed on the table only seconds before Lanier came into the room.

Lanier sat down. Picking up a slice of toast, she began eating fast.

"Slow down, girl." Ashleigh laughed. "If you're in that big of a hurry, take it with you. I'll pour your coffee into a travel cup."

"Thanks, Ash. I don't want to be late. Once I own the place, I won't have to deal with Casey. The final walk-through will be conducted by a building contractor."

"Same process we went through for Haven House." Standing at the sink, Ashleigh transferred coffee from a mug to a travel cup. When she turned around, she noticed Lanier looked troubled. "What's going on? You have an odd look on your face."

Lanier sighed hard. "I don't want to cancel my appointment, but I do want us to see Patricia as quickly as possible. It's the right thing to do. I hope you understand what I'm saying."

Ashleigh nodded. "I do. You should always come to your own conclusions. We can see Patricia later this afternoon. I'll make the call."

Lanier nodded. "Okay. I'll get back as soon as I can. See you then."

Ashleigh handed Lanier the coffee then hugged her. "Good luck this morning."

Lanier took a deep breath before she went into the complex office. When Casey wasn't at her desk, she nearly turned around and walked out.

"Hello, Lanier," Casey said, coming out of another office.

"Hello." Lanier didn't smile because she didn't feel charitable toward Casey.

"Are you ready to get down to business?"

"That's why I'm here," Lanier said in a clipped tone.

"Good." Casey pulled out a chair in front of her desk. "Have a seat. I'll go over all the paperwork with you. This is a lengthy process, but I'll make it painless. Did you bring the cashier's check?"

"It's covered." Lanier had gotten a bank check, but she hadn't filled it in yet. She had decided to wait until she made the purchase. She also wanted to hear the terms first.

Casey went behind her desk and sat down. She pulled Lanier's sales folder from the metal file slots on top of her desk. She scanned the contract quickly, having already read it thoroughly a couple of times.

Very plainly, Casey explained the terms of Lanier's town house purchase. She told her what interest rate she had been able to get her, saying that it was the lowest rate currently offered. The monthly amount of the house note was given to Lanier, which included principle and interest and homeowner's insurance was discussed in depth.

"I hope you're satisfied with the terms. As a homeowner himself, Mr. Carrington can probably assure you that you're getting a great deal. Your high credit score afforded you the lowest interest rate. You can now sign the contract and surrender the cashier's check for the down payment."

Lanier was annoyed. "What does Mr. Carrington have to do with this transaction? You keep bringing him up. Why?"

"I just thought the terms might matter to both of you, since you're exclusive."

"Our relationship has nothing to do with me purchasing a town house. I asked you to stay out of our private business, but you've ignored my request." Lanier got to her feet. "I'm not prepared to sign the contract today. I need more time to think about this, but it doesn't look good. I'm not sure I want to live in a place where my privacy is compromised by an employee."

Casey looked flabbergasted as Lanier made her

way to the exit. The astonished look gave way to an angry smile. "I can sue you for breach of contract," she shouted after Lanier.

Lanier stopped and turned around. "Sue me. Good luck with it, since I haven't signed a contract yet nor have I filled out the pay-to-the-order-of line on the cashier's check. Goodbye, Casey. I'm sure you'll figure it all out in time. You're a clever girl, but not a very bright one."

Inside her bedroom, Lanier stripped out of her business attire. She stepped inside the closet and put her clothing back on hangers. Before leaving the spacious closet, Lanier took down a pair of well-worn blue jeans and a short-sleeve white top. Locating her white tennis shoes, she picked them up and went back to the bedroom and dressed. She then sat down in the chair to put on her sneakers.

Lanier joined Ashleigh outside on the front porch swing. Both ladies acknowledged each other with a slight nod and a smile. They loved to sit on the porch and watch nature, and it was how they'd spend quiet time when the girls weren't present.

"How'd your meeting go, Lanier? Are congratulations in order?"

"It went badly, and there's nothing to congratulate me for. Casey brought up Dallas again, and it irritated me something awful. If she listens to her messages, she'll know that I have no intention of buying the town house from her. I don't need the aggravation."

"Lanier, why are you letting this woman get to you?

She probably mentions Dallas on purpose just to get you to react. Are you sure you don't want to purchase the town house?"

"Not one in that complex. There are a lot of brand-new town house properties around here. I don't want to deal with that woman another day. She says she's going to sue me."

"Sue you? Did you sign a contract and give her your down payment?"

"Neither. All she got was another taste of my attitude. She likes ticking me off."

"Are you sure you didn't sign anything?"

"Nothing at all."

"How'd she bring up Dallas?"

"Telling me he'd assure me of the great deal I got, since he's a homeowner. There was no reason for her to bring him up at all. I think she has a crush on him. I'm willing to bet on it. She thinks she's clever, but she's more overbearing than anything. And to think I liked her at first makes me feel foolish."

Ashleigh drew in fresh air through her nostrils. "I'm sorry for what you went through, and I'm glad you didn't sign anything or hand over any money. It sounds to me like you wouldn't have been happy there. This Casey person seems to be a thorn in your side."

"I loved the town house. It was beautiful. But my life is complicated enough without adding more complications. Casey Rayburn is a troublemaker. She comes off sweet at first, and then she goes on the attack. She caught me totally off guard the first time she asked me about Dallas."

"Let it go now. Rehashing it only gets you more

upset. We can look for another place whenever you're ready, but I'm not so sure you want to move away from Haven House. What will you do with your property if you and Dallas decide to marry?"

Lanier drew her legs up under her. "Dallas hasn't asked me to marry him again since I turned him down, but maybe getting a second residence isn't the best idea. Should he ask me to marry him we'd have too many properties to maintain." Lanier scowled hard.

"What's wrong? I know that look."

"I still wonder if I'm ready for marriage. I love Dallas enough to spend the rest of my life with him, but I still have lots of work to do on me."

"You can work on yourself while married. Give yourself a chance, and give Dallas a shot at being a very good husband to you. You two seem perfect for each other."

"We are, but I'm to blame for our problems. I keep thinking my marriage could end up like my parents' did. Loving Dallas is easy, but I'm afraid I'm still working on loving Lanier."

"Did you tell Dallas you were purchasing the town house?"

"I told him I put in an application. He may be disappointed that I backed out on the deal."

"Tell him, and then give him a chance to voice his thoughts on it. I don't know if he'll be disappointed in something you don't feel right about. So don't jump to any conclusions."

"Good advice, Ash. I'll do that." Lanier got a dreamy look in her eyes. "I wonder how many best girlfriends end up with two brothers, exact look-alikes. You're married to Austin and I hope to marry Dallas. What do you think about that?"

Ashleigh stood up. "Why don't we ask Dallas what he thinks? That's his car pulling in."

Lanier looked shocked. "Oh, no, please don't ask him that. I was just wondering. Why is he here? He rarely drops in without calling."

"Calm down, kid. I wouldn't think of asking him about that…and you know it."

Lanier didn't hear Ashleigh. She was too busy worrying why Dallas had dropped by unannounced. *Was something wrong with someone in his family?*

"Hey, Lanier, you look beautiful. Are you okay?"

"Of course I am. Why would you think I wasn't?"

Dallas shrugged. "You left your meeting before it was over."

"How'd you know about that?"

Dallas elevated an eyebrow. "I got there right after you left."

Lanier appeared annoyed. "Why were you there? How'd you know about the meeting?"

"Casey told me. She thought it was a good idea if I came there to support you."

"When did Casey tell you that?"

"I guess after the appointment was set up with you."

Lanier's forehead wrinkled. "You don't find that strange? I'm the one buying the town house. How did she get in contact with you?" Lanier's agitation was growing.

Dallas's brows furrowed. "She called my house."

Stunned, Lanier glared at him. "Why does she have your home number?"

"Hold on! Wait a minute. You're firing questions at me right and left. Did you put me down as a reference on your loan application?"

"I'd never give out your personal information. I purposely didn't use you as a reference. I'd never expose you to any type of sales people or to anyone else."

Ashleigh stepped off the porch as a van pulled onto the lot and parked. "Patricia is here, Lanier. Let's go meet her." Ashleigh gave Dallas a sympathetic glance.

"Good idea. Let's go." Lanier shot Dallas a dark look before turning on her heels and walking away. "Did you hear any of that?" she asked Ashleigh.

"I heard it all, Lanier. You *were* shouting. What do you think is going on?"

"He says Casey called him to come to our meeting. Why would she do that? We're not buying property together. This woman seems to have an agenda for Dallas. I won't rest until I get to the bottom of it. She's not getting away with her slick moves on him."

Ashleigh reached for Lanier's hand. "Put your business face on. The Social Service Department trusts us to take care of displaced kids," she whispered.

Smiling, Lanier slid her hand into Ashleigh's, squeezing gently. She then extended her hand to the social worker. "Hi, Patricia. Welcome back to Haven House. Come on in so we can start the meeting."

"Thanks, Lanier. I appreciate you and Ashleigh taking a last-minute appointment."

Ashleigh and Patricia followed along behind Lanier into the house.

Lanier thought hard about the situation with Casey

and Dallas. *Was he to blame for Casey's actions? Did he lead her on in some way?*

Lanier didn't know if Dallas had done something to encourage this kind of behavior or not. Perhaps he had unwittingly flirted with Casey. There was nothing unknowing about the wildly flirtatious way that he'd come at her on the cruise. His involvement was questionable, but Casey was definitely a culprit in this situation. Lanier was pretty sure of that. This woman had somehow gotten Dallas's home number, but it hadn't come from her.

Hearing Dallas's car engine start up had Lanier fighting off tears. She didn't turn around to look out the screen door, but she figured he was leaving. Instead of looking back, she moved farther into the house. Terribly grateful she'd left the meeting by the time Dallas had arrived, she sighed. She didn't want to even imagine the anger she more than likely would've expressed.

Dallas turned off his car a minute or two after Lanier was inside Haven House. He didn't want to leave things this way. A chill was lodged between them, and he didn't think either of them was responsible. None of it made any sense. And once again he needed clarity from her.

Settling his head back against the headrest, Dallas closed his eyes, thinking about how Lanier must feel. He had decided to stick around to find out if she was okay. Too many people had left her behind already. He hoped Lanier had settled down by the time the visitor had left. She was seriously angry, and he wondered if she knew how loud she'd been. If he got a chance to see her, he didn't want another verbal confrontation.

Ashleigh and Patricia walked out the front door.

Hearing the heavy door slam, Dallas opened his eyes. He watched the two women step off the porch. Were they heading toward him or to the van parked to the left of his car?

Ashleigh stopped at Dallas's car, motioning for him to roll down the window.

He did as he was asked. "Hey, Ashleigh, what's up?"

"Not much. We just had a meeting about taking in emergency placements. I'll talk to you about it after the social worker leaves. I'm glad you stayed. Lanier needs you. Go and see her."

"Ash, you know us so well," he said, laughing. Wasting no time, he rolled up the window and stepped out of the car. "You really think it's okay to go in? How do you think Lanier will react?"

"Come on, D., you know how to handle that little girl. She won't put up a fuss."

Inside the house, Dallas walked over to where Lanier sat. He knelt down before her.

"Want to talk about what happened?"

Lanier nodded. "We can talk upstairs in my bedroom, if you don't mind."

They climbed the stairs and went into her bedroom. Dallas sat on Lanier's bed, where he lodged his face in his hands.

Sensing that he was hurt, she felt even worse for how she'd reacted. Ashleigh didn't have to tell her how boisterous she'd gotten. Her voice had been full of anger, but had she been upset with the wrong person?

Lanier joined Dallas on the bed and put her arms around him. "Sorry about how I reacted. Was I wrong in blaming you for what occurred?"

"Dead wrong. The only part I played in it was filling out the visitors' card and leaving it with Casey. I must've put down my home telephone number without thinking. I'm surprised I even know my house number, since I always use the cell."

"I recall filling out one of those cards, too. But it doesn't mean employees can use that information however they choose. Casey obviously used it for the wrong reasons. Has she come on to you?"

"I haven't noticed anything out of the ordinary, not until now. I now realize I shouldn't have been asked to attend this meeting. I'm not the buyer. It sounds like something devious is going on, but she has no clue how hard I play ball. She won't get away with this."

"She's already gotten away with it. But the one thing she didn't plan on is me walking out." She paused for a moment. "Because I don't know her motivation for involving you, I wonder—have you led her to believe you were personally interested in her? Did you flirt with her or possibly give her the impression you were available to her?"

"You don't know the answer to your questions?" Dallas's eyes narrowed to thin slits. "I guess you don't. I thought you'd learned to trust me. It doesn't appear to be the case. It seems we're really making headway in our relationship, then it suddenly feels like we're back at square one. What do you want from this relationship? Better yet, what do you want from me?"

How many mistakes is it going to take for me to lose him altogether? She had to wonder.

Lanier got up and dropped down onto Dallas's lap. She kissed him deeply, and when he responded, she felt better.

Dallas couldn't help responding to Lanier's kisses, regardless of his level of frustration with her. "Can I get an answer to my questions?"

Lanier cradled her face in her hands, wishing she hadn't made him feel bad. "I want our relationship to work. Above all, I want your love."

"You have my love, but you don't act like you know it or believe in it. Our relationship can work if we both give it our all. I thought I was doing that."

"Dallas, you do give me your all. Perhaps I don't know how to fully receive it. I appreciate your love and patience, but I still allow the past to influence my reactions."

"The past is the past, Lanier. Either let go of it or continue to be controlled by it.

"Can you tell me why you left the meeting before it was over?"

Lanier looked down at the floor. "Didn't Casey tell you what happened?"

Dallas sighed hard. "I'm not asking Casey, Lanier. I'm asking you."

"I was sure I'd put her in her place the day she asked me if we were in a serious relationship. This new shenanigan tells me differently. She said that as a homeowner, you'd be able to tell me what a good deal I got on the loan. I asked her why she kept bringing you up to me. She tried to come off as astonished, but it was an act."

"That's *all* that happened?"

"You say that like you think it was a trivial matter. It wasn't unimportant to me."

"You're assuming again. Anyone who sees the way I look at you would know how serious we are."

Lanier blushed. "You say the sweetest things." She tenderly kissed his mouth. "Thanks for not leaving."

Dallas stood and brought Lanier up and into his arms. "Everything is fine. I'll make sure we keep it that way."

Looking up at him, she winked. "You're the one constant in my life. I'm glad I have you. I can't imagine being without you."

"Don't try to imagine it. I'm here for you whenever you need me or want me." He pressed his lips against her forehead. "Let's head back downstairs."

Lanier slid her arm around Dallas's waist and led him downstairs and steered him toward the kitchen.

Walking over to Ashleigh, Lanier hugged her. "I'm happy we both attended the meeting with Patricia. But, please, tell me anytime you think I'm making a bad decision. You don't steer me wrong."

Ashleigh laughed softly. "Don't want you to think I'm chastising you. Like I've said before, I want you to draw your own conclusions."

"She doesn't think that about you, Ash," Dallas chimed in. "She's happy for your love and guidance."

Lanier nodded. "He's right. I'm more grateful to you than you can imagine."

"We have each other's back, no matter what. You did a lot to help Austin and me to stay connected. When I wanted to give up on us as a couple, because of his ex-fiancée, you made me see that he wanted only me."

Dallas grinned. "I love you two just as you are." He looked toward the front door. "Let's sit on the porch. It's beautiful outside."

"I'll join you in a bit," Lanier said, and Dallas walked out.

Ashleigh put a finger to her temple. "I was thinking about something, Lanier. It's been a long time since we had a girls-only night. Maybe we should get together later on. A.C. is staying with his grandparents tonight."

"Sounds good to me, but I wouldn't dare pull you away from your husband. I'm sure Austin wants you at home with him."

"Austin likes to see me spend time with my friends."

Lanier nodded. "I know he does. Why don't we call Kelly and see if she can come? What do you think?"

Ashleigh grinned. "Awesome!"

Lanier glanced at the stove's clock. "Kelly should be in the office. Why don't we call her right now?"

"Great idea!" Picking up the wall phone, Ashleigh dialed Kelly's office.

Lanier listened in on Ashleigh's side of the conversation. By the smile on her face, it seemed things were going well. She thought it'd be nice to have friends over for an evening.

Lanier rarely let loneliness get her down anymore because she'd been lonely all her life. Like she'd done with everything else painful, she'd sucked it up. That's how she'd gotten from day to day. Still, she had to admit she'd been much less lonely over the past few years.

Ashleigh hung up. "Kelly's in. I'd better get out of here so I can take care of a few things I need to handle. I'll bring along a couple of movies, and I know you have all the latest music."

At the front door the two friends hugged, promising to see each other later.

Chapter 9

Dallas came up the walkway shortly after Lanier had exited the house. A warm feeling shot through her body; seeing him lifted her spirits.

A fleeting thought of having Dallas's babies whizzed through Lanier's mind, yet she couldn't conjure up an image of her belly bulging. Being a Carrington was a legacy in itself, since the name carried a lot of weight and expectations, especially in Texas. Lanier wasn't interested in the name, only in the man it belonged to. Walking to the edge of the porch, Lanier took hold of Dallas's arm. She kissed him and gave him a warm smile.

Back inside the house, the couple settled down in the family room. Dallas consulted his watch. "I've been here a long time."

"Is that a problem for you?"

"No, Lanier, it isn't. Why do you always go there?"

"Because I'm silly and immature." She looked apologetic. "I'm glad you're here. I love being in your company."

"That's more like it, babe. Thanks." He blew her a kiss. "However, I'll have to go shortly. There's a team meeting at five. We're having dinner and discussing strategies for our upcoming away game. Is there anything I can do for you before I leave?"

"Not really. I'm fine. I just plan to take a bath and relax. Ashleigh and Kelly are coming here to hang out this evening."

Dallas wore a mischievous grin. "I'd like to help you with that bath. Is that okay?"

"Sure." She smiled. "I'll go on up and run the water."

"We'll go upstairs together and I can help undress you." His smile was wickedly sexy.

"You're getting me hot over here. I'm sure that was your intention."

Dallas grinned. "No doubt about it. I am one lucky man and crazy about you."

"We're crazy about each other, Dallas. Ready to go up?"

"Ready as ever." He took her hand.

I can't wait to have a wife and then babies. I only want to father a child with the woman I love enough to marry. When will it happen for me? When will Lanier accept that she is the only one I've ever given my heart to?

Dallas was sure Lanier still wasn't ready to take the big plunge. He had to be blind to miss the signs. Her personal uncertainties had made him stop talking about marriage long ago. Yet he still constantly hoped for a miracle.

* * *

Lanier knelt down beside the tub and turned on the hot and cold water to reach the desired temperature. She liked her bath smoking hot. Getting up, Lanier walked over to the linen closet and pulled out a few towels. Once the tub was filled to her satisfaction, she turned to leave the bathroom.

Leaning on the door frame was Dallas, watching her every move, wearing an astonishing smile on his face. As he moved farther into the room, Lanier's heart careened. "Okay, baby, it's bath time."

Keeping his eyes fastened on her face, his hands went for her belt. Once her jeans were removed, he slid off her panties and then swept away her top. She wore no bra, which was a treat for him. Lifting her into his arms, he lowered her into the tub and knelt down beside it. Tenderly stroking Lanier's flesh with a white washcloth, Dallas was in heaven. His tenderness made her super hot for him. The steaming water was no match for his fire-breathing hands, and Lanier loved how they heated up her entire body.

"Can I impose on you to wash my hair, Dallas?"

Not wanting to miss out on a single second with Lanier, Dallas quickly retrieved the shampoo from a cabinet under the sink. He liked how sweet and soft her voice had been when she'd made her request. Dallas wished he could capture the loving expression that crossed her beautiful face.

After Dallas washed her hair and massaged her scalp, Lanier decided it was time to get out of the tub.

Once Dallas had her out, he wrapped a towel around her body and carried her into the bedroom. Lanier was drowsy and sexually aroused at the same time. After he laid her upon the bed, he grabbed a bottle of baby oil and began applying it to her skin.

"I hope my hands feel good to you. Relax and enjoy the master at work." Rubbing his hands together, he gave her a flirtatious smile.

Dallas squirted a good bit of lotion into his palms and rubbed them together, spreading it evenly on her skin. He massaged the soles of Lanier's feet and also tackled the flesh in between her toes.

Lanier pulled down Dallas's head and kissed him full on the mouth. "You're the man. I guess there's no end to your surprises."

Like an artist in the process of painting a priceless masterpiece, Dallas appeared intent on making every day special for them. Every time she smiled at him his ebony eyes shone with love and tenderness. She kept his world spinning.

Did Lanier see him as a hero? He wanted to be hers—and much more. What kind of future stories would they one day tell about their love? Would they be filled with love and joy, or pain and sorrow?

Dallas could only wonder.

Dallas hoped that his and Lanier's stories were nothing like the horrible ones she had from her childhood. It had taken her a long time to stand up and take ownership of the story about being removed from her family home. It had taken her an even longer time to feel at ease with a man. And not with just any man, Dallas knew. She had told him he was the only man who'd ever brought her peace.

After massaging in the last bit of lotion, Dallas lay down next to Lanier, mentally promising to always be right there to catch her should she fall.

Again and again, Dallas made Lanier feel as if she was the only woman in the world for him. He was the only man for her. She had showered with Dallas before, but he hadn't ever bathed her or washed her hair. They both knew it was special that she'd finally been able to surrender to his care.

Dallas tousled Lanier's wet hair. "Where's your blow dryer?"

Lanier gave him a flirtatious smile. "I can take care of it. I'd rather you take care of my other physical needs."

"And what might those be?"

"I want you to make love to me. I need you."

Rolling on top of her, he wrapped her in his arms. "You're a wonderful woman. You've taken exceptional care of the girls, and now you're sharing all your love with me. Do you know what a large capacity you have for loving unconditionally? If you don't know, I'll be right here to tell you. You are a remarkable woman, and I'm happy you love me."

Lanier silently rejoiced. There was nothing else to say; this was simply a moment to savor. Dallas had said how he felt about her ability to love…and he'd voiced it so beautifully. What more did she need to hear? There was nothing that could top this moment in time.

Dallas consulted his wristwatch. He had two hours or so to give to Lanier. Quickly stripping out of his clothes, he tossed them aside. Lanier was already nude and hot for him. All systems were on go.

* * *

Dallas was upset that his attention span was on zero. His mind kept reverting to the lovemaking he'd shared with Lanier. He had tried to call her before entering the restaurant, but the answering machine had come on.

His coaches and the manager demanded that all cell phones be turned off during meetings and other important business events, so he wouldn't get a chance to try again.

Rod Tillman, respected manager of the Texas Hurricanes, tapped his fork against a crystal goblet. "Team, glad you're all accounted for. It's nice to see everyone. We are so close to the big show. Are you guys beginning to smell victory?"

A round of applause broke out.

Tillman looked over at Dallas. "Carrington, your performance has been our saving grace lately, and you've brought us back from the brink of defeat the last few games. Can we let him know how much we appreciate his commitment to excellence?"

A standing ovation followed. He was the superstar, and no one minded giving him his props. Although he refused to wear that title, he knew he was an extraordinary player.

Dallas acknowledged his teammates with a huge smile. Holding his hands out, he gestured for everyone to sit. "Every single one of our wins has been a team effort. You guys deserve the same credit."

Dallas stood to address his teammates. "We can do this! As Mr. T. said, we're so close to winning the coveted pennant race. Personally, I can darn near taste it. If we sustain our level of play, the Texas Hurricanes will be in the World Series. Some of us have a ring, or rings...and some don't. Let's make sure our team walks away with the whole enchilada." Dallas sat down.

The Hurricanes' superstar pitcher, Manny Torres, stood. "I agree with Dallas. We haven't been this close to a pennant race win in three years. We all dream about the rings, which are important, but winning is everything. Let's keep a *yes we can* attitude."

The team was on a natural high, determined to go all the way. Everyone knew things didn't always turn out as planned, but there was no room for negative thinking.

Winning it all was the team's focus.

Lanier stood back and looked at her handiwork. She smiled, mentally giving herself a huge pat on the back. She'd been busy pulling together a light menu for an evening of fun with her girlfriends. The menu consisted of a tossed salad, homemade turkey and chicken salads on wheat rolls and glass platters of citrus fruits, apples and seedless grapes.

Lanier had wanted to bake a large batch of chocolate chip cookies, Ashleigh's favorites, but time ran out. Awakening from her nap a couple of hours ago, Lanier had hastily dressed in a pair of black jeans, a white polo and white sneakers. Dallas had given her a natural sleeping pill, the kind she loved. His lovemaking had been relaxing, but it had also left her craving more.

Lanier thought she heard the front door opening. It had to be Ashleigh. Running up front, she looked around for her friend, but the house was empty. "Maybe I'm hearing things."

While heading back to the kitchen, Lanier heard a loud noise and she turned around and faced the door. A big grin slowly spread across her lips. "Hey, I thought I'd heard someone."

"Sorry if I startled you," said Ashleigh. Dressed in impeccable casual attire and carrying several bags, Ashleigh moved into the hall. "I came inside a minute ago, but I went right back out for my purse. I'd left it in the car."

The two women went into the kitchen.

Moving over to the counter, Ashleigh began emptying the bags. "From the look of things, you have it all together, but I don't see any nuts, chips or dip. My trip to the grocery store has paid off. I bought a bunch of salty snacks."

"What time will Kelly get here?" Lanier asked Ashleigh.

Ashleigh began folding the empty bags. "She was on her way the last time we talked."

The doorbell rang and both women laughed.

Ashleigh grinned. "Your question is answered, unless you're expecting someone else."

"Only you and Kelly," Lanier responded.

The two women went out into the hallway and headed for the front door, which Lanier opened for Kelly. "Hey, girl, how are you?"

Kelly smiled warmly. "I'm fine, thanks."

"Glad to see you," Lanier said. She drew in Ashleigh and Kelly for a group hug.

The party of three settled into the family room, chatting away and laughing at each other's silly jokes and remarks. They were so caught up with discussing recent happenings in each other's lives that an hour and a half passed by with lightning speed.

Kelly stood. "Excuse me. I'll be right back. I need to get something out of my car."

"Need some help?" Ashleigh asked.

"It's just a couple of light packages. I'll only be a minute or two." Kelly took off running.

Lanier looked at Ashleigh. "Are you hungry?"

"Close to starving," she confessed. "I've barely eaten a thing today. I have to start eating for two again, and staying so busy isn't an excuse."

Kelly returned with a shopping bag in her hand.

"I brought presents for you guys," Kelly announced cheerfully. She dug into her shopping bag and came up with two beautifully wrapped boxes. She handed one to each of her friends. "Hope you like what I chose."

Ashleigh took her time removing the wrapping paper, but Lanier ripped off her paper in one fell swoop. Pushing aside tissue paper, Lanier gasped with pleasure. The pure white silk gown and matching robe looked priceless and elegant. She removed the lingerie and saw that it was floor length.

Seeing Lanier's gift had Ashleigh hastening to open hers. She whistled. "Is this too hot or what? Austin is going to love me in this red daredevil nightgown. He might let me keep this one on my body a little longer than normal. Sometimes I don't know why I bother to wear nightclothes to bed."

Lanier grinned. "You know why. Stripping away your clothing can get pretty erotic."

"That's an understatement," Kelly remarked. "I loved

the gowns enough to buy one of each for myself in nude and basic black."

Lanier smiled. "Thanks a bunch, Kelly. It was thoughtful of you to bring gifts."

Ashleigh waved her hand. "I second that! My gown is stunning. I'm eager to see Austin's expression when I wear it. Thanks so much."

"You're both welcome. It was my pleasure," Kelly said.

"The food is ready to serve," Lanier announced. "If you guys go into the dining room, I'll bring everything in there. I made a pitcher of regular iced tea and an herbal one for you, Ash. Does anyone want something other than tea?"

Both women shook their heads.

"I'm going to put on some music," Kelly announced. "I'm in the mood for salsa. Is that okay with everyone?" Once she got the approval from her hosts, Kelly thumbed through the Latin selections.

Ashleigh put the gowns back in their boxes and laid them aside. She was glad Lanier was ready to serve dinner. She was way too hungry.

Finished with the light meal, Lanier glanced around the table. This was the first time in a long while that the threesome had gotten together for an evening of chitchat and fun. It had taken a few hours to pull together the light feast, yet it had been polished off in mere minutes. There was no doubt in Lanier's mind that everyone had enjoyed the food.

"It's time for dessert. Let's eat it in the family room. Coffee?" Lanier inquired.

Kelly held up a finger. "Please, black for me."

Ashleigh stood to begin clearing the table. "You ladies go on into the family room. I'll take care of the coffee after I tidy up things a bit."

Lanier leapt to her feet. "Not a chance, girl. I want you and your precious baby on board to go sit in your favorite recliner and get comfortable. Put up your feet and relax. I'll make the java. Skedaddle, ladies. I'll be along in a few."

Kelly stood, playfully bumping Lanier's shoulder with hers. "We'll get this done much faster as a team. Then we can get into the latest Hollywood rumors."

Everyone laughed. Ashleigh hugged her partners in crime before vacating the room.

Kelly stacked dirty dishes, saucers, serving bowls and platters and carried them into the kitchen. She loved this dining room and would've decorated hers in a similar fashion had she seen it before her house was built.

Kelly retrieved a lemon meringue pie from the refrigerator and sliced the entire pie and transferred the slices to dessert plates.

"Better add another sliver of pie to Ashleigh's plate. She loves lemon meringue."

Kelly grinned. "Got it!"

Since Ashleigh didn't drink anything with caffeine while pregnant, Lanier retrieved a carton of cold soy milk and poured a full glass, and when the coffee was ready, they carried everything into the family room.

Ashleigh looked up from the newspaper she held when her friends entered. Watching as Kelly and Lanier laid out items on the coffee table, she knew it'd do no good to try to help. Lanier poured coffee into two cups and handed one to Kelly. Picking up the glass of soy milk, she handed it and a fancy paper napkin to Ashleigh.

Ashleigh smiled. "You remember everything, don't you?"

Lanier smiled back. "Just the important stuff. Half the time I can't remember my name."

"Speaking of names, have you and Austin picked one for the baby yet?" Kelly asked.

"We've tossed around quite a few, but we haven't settled on anything definite. If it's a girl, we've seriously discussed naming her after my maternal grandmother, Ireland. I found her name while I was researching my family tree."

"Ireland Carrington is rich and classy. I love it," Lanier remarked, loving the beautiful name. "What about a boy?"

"Austin likes London. I like Taylor." Ashleigh chuckled.

"London and Ireland," Kelly remarked. "If you keep that trend, you'll have a little United Kingdom running around your place. The guys are named after Texas cities, so I'm surprised Austin isn't sticking with family tradition."

"Oh, I beg to differ," said Ashleigh. "San Antonio Carrington has come up. Laredo is another one mentioned for a boy or girl. I'm not fond of either, but I'll go along with whatever Austin wants. I just hope he doesn't decide on El Paso or Lubbock. Dallas said to go with

Tejas, which is based on the Caddo word for Texas. Can you imagine using all three names if I have triplets?"

The ladies had a good laugh over Ashleigh's comment.

"I promise to let you know our final decision. We have seven months to get it right. I'd love a girl, but all I want is a healthy baby." Ashleigh glanced at Kelly. "A wedding date yet?"

Kelly's smile beamed. "We're thinking about this Christmas Eve. You and Austin got married on Christmas Eve, and the truth of the matter is that the guys had always talked of having a triple wedding. Houston wants to get married on the same day as you and Austin."

Ashleigh clapped her hands. "That's wonderful! We'd love to share an anniversary with you two. Maybe Austin and I can renew our vows at the same time. His mom always dreamed of her sons sharing one wedding date."

Lanier wished she could disappear. She and Dallas were nowhere near ready to revisit wedding plans, yet he wanted to be married. Sure that she was holding him back, her heart lurched painfully.

Ashleigh instantly noticed Lanier's melancholy expression. "Honey, I'm sorry if we upset you. We'd never do anything to hurt you." Ashleigh came over and sat down next to Lanier and gave her a tender hug. "You can have the same wedding day, too, if you want it. Dallas would marry you in a heartbeat. He loves you so much, Lanier. You have to feel his love."

Kelly felt awful. She crossed the room and settled down at Lanier's feet. "Ashleigh's right, you know.

Dallas is ready for happily ever after. Have you two discussed marriage?"

Lanier wiped away tears at the corners of her eyes. "Dallas used to talk about it, but he no longer brings it up. I get too upset. Why am I so abnormal? Every woman wants to get married and live happily ever after with the man she loves, but just the thought of it terrifies me. Yet I couldn't love Dallas more."

"Lanier, there's no other woman for Dallas Carrington. He's told us that time and time again. Do you want to marry him?" Kelly asked.

"Of course I do. But when you come from a background as horrendous as mine, how do you even entertain the idea of forever? My parents got addicted to drugs and alcohol and let their child be taken away. They're remarried now, but they were divorced. Dallas doesn't want just a wife, he wants babies, too. He'd love to have four or five kids. I'd love kids someday, but what happens to them if I turn out like my own parents? You tell me."

Ashleigh put her arm around Lanier, hoping to calm her. "Sweetie, don't do this. You *are not* your parents. You're *not* responsible for their atrocious conduct. Have you thought of going back to your therapist?"

Lanier shook her head. "The woman has more problems than me. She tells me her sob stories before I get a chance to tell mine. She's had a bad upbringing…and shares many of my fears, including a fear of marriage. Maybe I need a new therapist."

Ashleigh kissed Lanier's cheek. "Get a new therapist. Do whatever it takes to have the life you've dreamt of. Dallas loves you. He can give you anything you want."

Lanier nodded. "I know." She frowned. "Let's just change the subject, if you don't mind. We got together to enjoy an evening of fun."

Ashleigh and Kelly agreed to change the topic of their discussion.

Chapter 10

A beautiful day in late September was just what Lanier needed to cheer her up. She had awakened feeling good. The trees on the property had changed to bold gold, browns, reds and reddish-yellows. It seemed to her as if she had waited forever to see the colors of autumn in full bloom. Spring bulbs had already been planted for next year.

The young foster females had come back from camp for a brief stay. Lanier and Ashleigh had purchased new clothes and shoes for them to take along to college. Dallas and Austin had surprised the young ladies with a new SUV to drive to Southern Methodist University, where they'd been accepted. They'd left a few days early to get settled in.

The hoopla of the past couple of weeks still hadn't come to an end. The Texas Hurricanes were in first place in their division, poised to take it all. Dallas was currently on the road with his team. He'd been gone several days and was due to return home soon. Lanier missed him, but she'd grown used to his absences during baseball season. Knowing her answer would be no or "I can't," he'd stopped inviting her to come with him.

Waiting on her mother to show up for lunch, Lanier paced the living room floor, looking out the picture window every five seconds. She felt totally unnerved. A showdown was imminent. Lanier had tried to put the meeting off until later since she hadn't come up with all the questions she wanted to ask. Quite a few of her queries desperately needed answers. If she could get over her past, she'd stand a better chance of dealing with the present. Then she could finally begin planning a real future with Dallas.

Lunch was ready and was being kept warm on a low temperature in the oven. Lanier had prepared cube steak and gravy with mushrooms and onions. Angelica had come by earlier to see how Lanier was doing. As a gift to her son's love interest, she'd brought a dozen yeast rolls fresh from her oven. The Carrington parents were extremely fond of Lanier.

Back in the kitchen, Lanier checked on her meal. Lowering the oven door, she slid back the aluminum foil and peered down on the meat. Before she'd put the foil back in place, the doorbell pealed.

Lanier looked panic-stricken. "She's here," she said to herself. "Please let me get through this visit. I badly want a relationship with my parents and to be able to move on with my life."

Moving at a snail's pace, Lanier made her way to the front door, wishing Dallas was there for her. The man did wonders for her disposition. She truly missed him, though she'd seen him several nights in a row before his departure. Lanier planned to spend a lot more quality time with him so they could get on with their future.

Lanier slowly inched the front door open, wishing she were anywhere but there. "Mom," she greeted, smiling weakly.

Barbara's features appeared strained. "Is it really this hard to be around me?"

"The truth? It is harder than anything I've ever done," Lanier confessed.

Taking hold of her daughter's hand, Barbara lifted it to her lips. "I understand. The hardest thing I've ever done was forgetting I was a mother. I let a whiskey bottle and other substances come between my daughter and me. Can I please come in so we can talk? I won't stay long. We can save lunch for another visit."

"Lunch is ready." Lanier stepped aside. "We can go into the family room to talk first." Lanier wanted to get this conversation over with.

As Barbara followed Lanier, she bit down on her lower lip. Knowing she'd never comprehend the depth of pain her daughter had suffered at her own parents' hands, she didn't blame Lanier for how she felt. She just hoped to salvage their relationship.

Lanier waited until her mother was seated before she sat down next to her. Wringing her hands together, she thought of the most important questions to ask first.

Barbara hated seeing Lanier struggling this way.

"You can ask me anything. I'll give you the truth. I owe you that much, Lanier."

"I guess I just want to know…why? Why did you allow me to stay in the foster care system? Why didn't you come back for me or come to visit me wherever I was?"

Barbara folded her hands. "So much went on back then. Your dad and I were locked up for a short time because we didn't have money to post bail. I didn't know where they'd taken you. When I did find out, I didn't go see you right away…and you were gone from there by the time I visited. The cycle of finding you had to start all over again."

Lanier's eyes blurred with tears. "Why didn't you ever find me?"

"I stopped trying. Just like your dad, I was an addict. It numbed the horrific pain but only for a brief time. Joseph was abusing alcohol before you were taken. He wanted me to have a drink with him or hit a joint, and I did it because I wanted to keep him home. I feared he'd get himself killed hanging out in the streets. I had forsaken all that I was and all that I had to keep my marriage intact. After I began using frequently, I no longer considered you, period. That's a terrible thing for a mother to say to her only child, but it's the truth."

Lanier could only stare at her mother. The truth hurt way more than she'd thought it would, yet she was glad it had been told. All the fear she'd had about being a mother was still with her, but she knew she'd never mistreat a child. Abandoning her flesh and blood was out of the question.

"So drugs and alcohol meant more to you than I did, the baby you birthed?"

"Your dad meant more to me than anything in this world. I was out there with him because I loved him more than life. Did I make wrong choices? You bet."

The words Barbara had spoken cut into Lanier's heart like a surgeon's scalpel. "It's nice that you can admit it, but it doesn't do me a lot of good."

"None of what I've done has done you any good. Every choice I made was wrong. You should've come first in my life. I only missed you when I became clean and sober. It was then that I realized what I'd done to you. It still took me a long time to come to terms with it enough to try and see you. Saying I'm sorry will never be enough, but I am terribly sorry."

Lanier's tears spilled over. Her face was wet, but she didn't wipe it. "Your honesty hurts more than I imagined. At least you've been truthful. Why *did* Dad start using?"

"Losing his job to someone younger was a strain on him. It was difficult to work under someone you'd supervised. The first odd thing I noticed was him drinking beer, something he'd never bothered with. He quickly graduated to wine and on to hard liquor. I honestly can't tell you when the drugs started because he was drinking at the same time. I do recall the first time he asked me to smoke—"

Lanier held up her hand in a halting gesture. "I don't need to know the name of the substances you abused. It won't change a thing. You've told me why you chose your husband over me. That's enough for me to get used to. Mom, you have no idea what horrific treatment I received in foster care. I experienced horrible nightmares, but I'm not there anymore. I'm an adult, a successful one. I have a master's degree in social work. That's my truth."

"I'm proud of you, Lanier. You're doing very well and I'm happy for you. Don't let what your father and I did keep you bitter. You are your own woman. You get to call all the shots in your life. I never had it like that until recently. I counted on your father for everything. When it looked like I was losing him, I joined him to keep him."

Wrapping her arms around Barbara's neck, Lanier hugged her tightly. "I still don't understand how you did it, but you've obviously come to terms with yourself. If God can forgive you, who am I not to? Forgiveness doesn't necessarily mean we'll have this great relationship, but I'm willing to try."

Barbara squeezed her daughter. "Thank you, sweetheart. We need you in our lives."

Lanier suddenly pulled away. "To be honest, I don't know if I can have a relationship with Joseph. I blame him more than anyone. If he hadn't started using, we may not have been forced apart. I try hard to remember he's my father, but I can't recall anything good about him."

"That's 'cause bad stuff overshadows good. He is a good man, even if you only remember him as an addict. Right after our court date for the divorce, he asked me to have lunch with him. I couldn't resist him. I still can't."

Lanier appeared confused. "What happened after that?"

"We saw each other off and on for about a year before we remarried. We both went through rehab on our own, long before any court date. Please, Lanier, don't be too hard on him. He's very aware of his wrongdoings, and he wants a relationship with his daughter. Take all the time you need to think it over. Joseph is back to being the kind, considerate man I fell in love with. I'm sorry you can't remember him like that."

"I'm sorry, too, Mom. I'm not closing the door on him, but there's only a fraction of a crack left open. It may or may not widen enough for him to enter. We have to wait and see. You came for lunch, and I cooked a great meal. Let's eat."

"Are you sure you want me to stay, Lanier?"

"I'm positive. I hope you'll love what I fixed."

"I'm sure I will. Want to give me a hint what it is?"

Lanier's lashes lowered momentarily. "Remember my favorite when I was younger?"

"Cubed steak and gravy."

Grateful that Barbara had remembered, Lanier smiled and nodded.

During the road trip, Dallas's team had won the coveted pennant race for the American League's Central Division. A huge party in their honor was to take place on a Saturday evening on the second weekend in October. The festivities would be held on a huge Texas estate belonging to the owner of the Hurricanes. Dallas had invited Lanier as his date, and his family was also attending.

Seated in a leather recliner in his family room, Dallas had mail scattered all about him. He had arrived home a couple of hours ago. Getting through the mail was a chore he hated, so he tackled it first. He picked up yet another pink envelope, wondering what she had to say now.

He sighed with disinterest as he read the latest note from her. The scent on the envelope didn't turn him on in the least, and he wasn't impressed with anything she'd written. It scared the daylights out of him when he read that the day they would be meeting was close at hand. He'd have to alert security not to let anyone inside the gates but the people who were already on his visitors list. The mystery woman's threat of a visit had gotten to him.

A lightbulb suddenly came on inside his head. Tossing the note aside, he got up from the recliner and strode back to his bedroom. Picking up his wallet and car keys, and moving rather quickly, he headed for the garage. He pressed a remote to the garage door, fired up the engine and backed his car out.

Casey was at her desk when Dallas walked in. A couple occupied chairs in front of her desk, so he began looking at the complex model on the wall. There weren't many home sites left. He was aware that Lanier had scrapped her plans to purchase the town house because of Casey's intrusion into her personal life.

Dallas had had mixed emotions about Lanier moving away from Haven House. More than anything, he wanted to marry Lanier and have her move into his home. Or they could rent out his place and pick out a new residence together. But if they weren't of one accord, marriage and a home together wasn't happening.

Fifteen minutes had lapsed when Casey walked up beside Dallas. She gave him a gleaming smile. "It's nice to see you. How are you?"

"Just fine, thank you. I won't stay long. I came to see if you're really ready to reveal yourself. Your last note seems that you are."

Casey's face lit up like a Christmas tree. "How did you guess?"

"Oh, a few things helped me figure it out. Why did you feel you had to resort to that odd method?"

"I don't know. It seemed like an intriguing way for you to get to know me better."

"You'd met me. I've been here several times already. I came alone the first time. The next time I brought along the woman I'm crazy about, the woman I plan to marry."

Casey looked as if she wished she could disappear. "Are you truly in love with Lanier?"

"Oh, you have no idea how much I love her. What made you think you could come between us?"

"Don't you think you deserve more than what she can give you? She seems cold."

A vein throbbed in Dallas's neck. "How do you know what she can or can't give me?"

"I've seen how timid she is. She acts like she's scared of her own shadow. Are you attracted to weakness? If so, Lanier is perfect for you. But I don't think she's what you want. You're too strong of a man to want an emotionally weak woman."

Dallas's eyes glowed with hot flames of anger. "Casey Rayburn, you may think you get us, but you don't. Do you like your job?"

"I love my job. It pays extremely well. I invest a lot of what I make in real estate. By my fortieth birthday, I plan to retire a millionaire."

"Sounds to me like you suffer from the pronoun *I*. Do you want to keep this job?"

Trying to ignore his cutting insult, Casey rolled her eyes. "Of course I want to keep it. Why wouldn't I?"

"If that's the case, you need to stop sending those little notes. You used my private information for your sick pleasure. I don't give my phone number and my address out to just anyone. I'm sure the 'powers that be' at your company don't sanction criminal behavior from employees."

"Criminal? Oh, please, you can't be serious!" She paused. "You'd take this situation to corporate? I can't believe you'd want me to lose my job."

"No more than you want me to lose the woman I love. If Lanier saw those notes, she wouldn't understand, and if she knew they came from you, you'd need to find a good hideout. Lanier is not someone you want to mess with. She'd be within her rights to let you have it."

Casey choked back her tears and disappointment. "I'm sorry…Dallas."

"Mr. Carrington to you—and please don't forget it. Consider yourself warned. If anything out of the ordinary happens again, you're the first person I'll blame. Since you've already lost the sale with Lanier, you'd better be thankful for that miracle."

"She walked out on our deal. When I finally got a

hold of her, I asked her to consider changing her mind about the purchase. She said, 'No sale,' then hung up on me. That should tell you everything. I'm sorry I lost a commission check, but maybe it's for the best. It'd be hard to see you and her around the property." She threw up her hands at his stern look. "Just being honest."

Fuming inside, Dallas turned on his heels and walked out.

Outside, where a cool evening breeze stirred mildly, Dallas stopped to catch his breath. He'd had enough of Casey Rayburn. It seemed as if she'd 'starting setting him up from the first day he'd visited the complex.

Whether to tell Lanier about Casey's notes weighed heavily on him. His lady had a hot temper and her buttons were easily pushed. He didn't think she'd physically harm anyone, but her tongue was dangerous. He'd given Casey good advice when he'd said that Lanier was not someone to mess with. It was up to Casey to heed the warning.

Dallas understood women being attracted to him, but there was no excuse for anyone to take a crush this far. Casey wasn't his type of woman. He wouldn't have dated her even if he hadn't been in love with Lanier. Dallas couldn't believe he hadn't suspected Casey long before now.

Making sure his Bluetooth was turned on, he punched in the number for Haven House. He was hoping he could see Lanier this evening.

"Hey, beautiful, it's me. I made it back home a few hours ago. What're you up to?"

Enchanted by Dallas's voice, Lanier smiled. "Welcome home! I'm stretched out reading a good novel. What's up with you?"

"Calling to find out if I can drop by to see my favorite girl."

"I'd love to see you. Have you eaten yet?"

"I grabbed a bite to eat with a few of the guys right after we landed. I can be there in about twenty minutes or so. Need anything?"

"Just you. See you soon, Dallas."

"Goodbye, sweetheart."

As soon as Lanier hung up the phone, it rang again. Thinking Dallas was calling back, she rapidly picked up the receiver. "Hey."

"Miss Watson, this is Casey Rayburn. I'm calling because I just had a talk with Dallas. I found it strange that he wasn't sure if you're purchasing a home with me or not. What's that about?"

"Casey, I made myself clear to you. I didn't purchase a town house in your complex because of your unprofessional behavior."

"You didn't change your mind because of Dallas, did you?"

Lanier frowned. "Again, what does Dallas have to do with it?"

"Everything! I guess he hasn't told you about the countless passes he's made at me. It started the first day he came in to see our models. We've been exchanging flirtatious emails and intimate notes and texts ever since. If you haven't gotten wind of it, you got it now."

Lanier's eyes filled with rage. "You've got to be crazy, lady, if you expect me to believe the crap you're spewing out. I know Dallas a lot better than you give me credit for. If he were interested in any other woman, he'd be honest about it right away."

"You think so, huh? Ask him about our flirtatious exchanges. If you know him so well, you'll know whether he's lying or not. Sorry to burst your bubble, but your man is not exclusively yours. Tell Dallas hello for me." Knowing she'd said more than enough to boil Lanier's blood, Casey disconnected.

Looking dumbfounded, Lanier just lay there on her bed, staring up at the ceiling.

Can I drop by to see my favorite girl?

Lanier replayed Dallas's remarks in her head several times over. If she wasn't his girl, he surely had made a fool of her. All this time he'd made her believe they were exclusive.

If Casey is telling the truth, it means that Dallas has been lying to me. No, he's not that kind of guy. Casey is just trying to pull another fast one. Losing a sale isn't anything to take lightly. No sale, no commission.

Lanier didn't know what to do. Should she confront Dallas with Casey's tale or just let it slide? If he wasn't guilty of anything, he'd think she didn't trust him— and that anyone would be able to come between them. Dallas had worked hard on getting her to trust him. It didn't make sense for him to betray her.

Getting up from the bed, Lanier went into the closet and pulled down a white sweater and a pair of eggplant-colored jeans. After tossing the clothing onto the bed, she stepped into the bathroom. Although she'd had a shower shortly before Dallas had called, she wanted to freshen up a bit.

* * *

A half hour later, Lanier was startled by the doorbell.

So many things had trooped through Lanier's head while she'd been waiting for Dallas. One thing was for sure. If she said something accusatory, and he was innocent, she'd end up losing him. His patience had to be running thin with her.

Making her way to the door, Lanier felt sick to her stomach. Even if she believed wholeheartedly in Dallas, and she did, Casey had created issues for them. Asking Dallas about Casey without offending him would be hard.

Lanier opened the door to Dallas. He immediately drew her into his arms and kissed her forehead. No matter how much she believed in him, she still found herself asking if it could be true.

Dallas presented Lanier with a red rose. "It hasn't fully bloomed yet."

She put the rose up to her nose and inhaled its perfumed scent. "Thank you. It's beautiful. Have a seat while I get a bud vase."

Dallas instantly sensed that something was wrong with Lanier. Her voice was shaky. When he'd held her, her body had trembled. Instead of continuing to analyze her, he went into the family room. Whatever it was it would come to light.

Filling the vase with water, Lanier centered the rose. She inhaled its scent again. How many nights had she dreamed of following a trail of rose petals that led to the man of her dreams?

Lanier was a dreamer, but she could also be a realist. *And reality could hurt.*

Dallas's eyes were closed when Lanier returned. Instead of disturbing him, she studied him closely. He was a fine male specimen. His ebony eyes had told her so many things, including how much he loved her. Those strong, toffee-brown arms had held her tight, keeping her safe and secure. His juicy lips brought her pleasure each time they united with hers. As her eyes dropped down, she gasped, remembering the feel of his manhood deep inside her.

To hell with Casey Rayburn.

Until Dallas gives me a reason to believe he's cheating on me, no one will run me off. I love him more than I ever dreamed possible. And my instincts tell me he loves me every bit as much as I love him. It's possible he loves me even more than I think.

Lanier quietly backed out of the room and went upstairs.

After retrieving the silk nightgown and robe Kelly had given her, Lanier stripped out of her clothes, replacing them with the hot, sexy gift. She let down her hair and brushed it briskly so it would fall about her shoulders. She sprayed her neck and other pulse points with her favorite perfume. She slipped her satin slippers on and went back downstairs.

Wide awake, Dallas whistled. "Wow! Don't know what I did to deserve this, but I'm thrilled." He stood and strode over to Lanier. Lifting her chin with two fingers, he planted a juicy kiss onto her lips. "You look stunning! And we're home alone. I can't wait to have you."

"Stop talking and get on with it," she said sassily.

He grinned. "You don't have to tell me twice."

Dallas carried Lanier over to the sofa and sat her down. Kneeling down in front of her, he brought her face to him and kissed her hungrily. His hand slid under her gown and met with bare skin. He tenderly fondled her breasts. She smelled so good, and he knew her perfume would linger on him for a long time afterward.

Dallas freed her breasts from his hand and imprisoned one with his mouth. Suckling her twin mounds, he felt his manhood expanding. It was too soon to end the foreplay they both wanted more of. His hands moved downward. Pushing up the gown, he caressed her bare thighs, massaging her soft flesh with gentle fingers. He nudged her knees apart with his own then inserted his fingers into her moist femininity, causing her to moan lustily. The sounds coming from deep inside her heightened his desire. Lanier squirmed and gasped as his hot hands roamed over her bare, feverish flesh.

"Lanier, Lanier, I need you so badly. You drive me crazy. I love you, baby."

Lanier couldn't utter a single word. Dallas's sweetly tortuous foreplay had rendered her speechless. She wanted him inside of her so bad it hurt. Her body's desire for release was insane.

With his lips locked onto hers, Dallas took out his wallet and fumbled around for a condom. He unzipped his slacks and took them off along with his briefs. He sheathed his manhood quickly and turned to her.

Spreading apart Lanier's legs and bringing her buttocks to the very edge of the sofa, Dallas slowly entered her, shuddering from pure desire. With his knees resting firmly on the carpet, Dallas began thrusting, making Lanier cry out from sheer pleasure.

Lanier squeezed his manhood from within and Dallas gasped. As she clenched and unclenched her muscles, he fought even harder to hang on. "Oh, Lanier, you have no idea how good you make me feel…"

Shushing him with her mouth, her tongue coiled around his. The uncontrollable feelings washing over her were almost too hot to handle. Riding atop the wild jerking motions of her body, Lanier closed off her mind, enjoying every second of the powerful climax roaring through her. Her wild shuddering caused her to dig her fingernails into Dallas's back.

With his manhood about to burst, Dallas deepened his thrusts, turning himself loose on her with a fury. "Lanier, I can't hold out any longer."

His body bucked and trembled and his release was beyond intense. As he lay still inside of her, he stroked the length of her hair. "I don't know how I'm going to find strength to pull myself up."

"Just lay within me until you feel stronger. You're spending the night with me, aren't you?"

"I don't want to be anywhere else."

Removing an afghan from the sofa back, Lanier covered Dallas and they snuggled close on the sofa. What he really wanted them to do was climb the stairs and fall into bed together, but he'd have to wait for more strength to come.

Lanier laid her head on his chest. "Are you satisfied?"

"I couldn't be more satisfied. Girl, you wore this

brother out. Being inside of you is a feeling I can't describe."

"That's good to hear. It's important for me to know I satisfy you. If I don't, you just might go elsewhere."

Dallas turned his head. "Is that what you think? Why would you believe I'd go somewhere else when it's only you I love and only you I make love to?"

"That didn't come out right. I don't know how to make it sound right. I hurt you, and I'm sorry."

"Lanier, I'm not hurt. I'm disappointed. I do everything in my power to let you know you're the only one, yet you still doubt me. Why?" The hurt in his voice was unmistakable.

"I don't doubt your love, Dallas. I see the effort you put into making me feel loved. Please charge it to my head and not my heart. Can you do that?"

Dallas raised an eyebrow. "Don't I always?"

Lanier smiled. "You've got a point. I'm thirsty. Want something to drink?"

"I'll get it. A Diet Coke?"

"You got it! I'm going upstairs to shower. Do you mind bringing the drinks up?"

"Not at all. Want some company in the shower?"

Lanier grinned, her eyes flashing flirty signals. "You know it. I'll wait for you."

Dallas smiled. "You won't have long to wait."

Knowing his strength hadn't returned full-force, Dallas waited until Lanier disappeared before he put on his briefs. It would've embarrassed him if he had trouble getting up from the sofa. Once they got married, he thought any and all embarrassment would go away.

Once we get married. Is that ever going to happen for us?

Out in the kitchen, Dallas removed two Cokes from the refrigerator.

As he headed toward the staircase, he laughed, shaking his head. His legs were still weak and wobbly from such a powerful climax. For an athletic man of his weight and stature, he should be able to run a marathon after any type of activity. Of course, other activities didn't cause his body fluids to drain completely.

One step at a time, man. Lanier's waiting.

After setting the sodas and a glass of ice on a nightstand, Dallas stripped down again.

Not wanting to waste a moment of his time with Lanier, he joined her in the shower. She was already squeaky clean but eager to get her hands on his body. She poured a generous amount of shower gel onto the bath sponge and began to play.

Because Lanier was dead tired, she had no plans to draw out the shower. It was still early, but she was ready to hit the sack. She didn't necessarily have to fall asleep, but she wanted to get comfortable. Lanier looked forward to turning on the television or the radio and just lying in bed until she fell asleep. When she was with Dallas, she loved nothing more than to lie in his arms and listen to his beating heart.

Unable to fall off to sleep, Dallas rolled onto his side. He was surprised to find Lanier still awake and he looked down into her eyes. "I have something important to say," said Dallas. "It's about Casey Rayburn, from the town house complex."

Lanier momentarily froze in her spot. "I know who she is. What about her?"

"She's a troublemaker. She thought she was being mysterious or something and started sending notes to my house, referring to herself as a secret admirer. I only figured out today that it had to be her. The only time I recall giving out my home address is when I filled out that visitors' card."

Lanier hushed Dallas with two of her fingers to his lips. "Let's not waste another moment on Casey Rayburn. She's not a part of our future. I'm not buying one of her townhomes, so we never have to see her again. As for us, think we can go another round?"

Dallas still felt too weak to make love to Lanier again. Swallowing his pride was easy because he could be up front with her without her ridiculing him. "Girl, I love the way you turn on this big guy, but I'm bone tired. I've spent a good deal of this day on a plane. Then I rushed over here to see you. Think I can get a rain check?"

She leaned down and kissed his mouth softly. "Hate to admit it, but I'm bushed, too. All I could think about was getting in this bed while we were in the shower. Rain check granted."

Lanier fell asleep right away, but Dallas was having a hard time with it. He couldn't stop thinking about Lanier's response when he told her about Casey. Her lips had told him not to waste any more time on Casey, but her demeanor said otherwise. This wasn't the last he'd hear about it, he guessed. As he'd already told the young woman, Lanier wasn't someone to mess with. The look he saw in her eyes had revealed her true feelings about Casey.

Chapter 11

The party held in honor of the Hurricanes' megawin was in full swing. The team had won big, beating their opponents by six runs. Dallas had popped two homers in the late innings, making them his second and third home runs of the evening.

Lanier wore a Vera Wang winter-white gown that was a vision of pure elegance. The formfitting gown clung like a second skin to her beautiful body. A sheer white silk shawl rested beside her. Sparkling shoes and an accentuating clutch were perfect complements for the designer gown. The solitaire pear-shaped diamond pendant and matching brilliant earrings she wore sparkled with pizzazz.

Seated quietly on a chair in a corner, Lanier's eyes darted everywhere, drinking in all the activities unfolding inside the beautifully decorated ballroom of a private mansion belonging to the owner of the Texas

Hurricanes. Lanier had been to many social affairs with Dallas, but this was by far the most upscale and largest event to date. He had told her that over five hundred people were invited to the party, and he couldn't imagine anyone had sent their regrets.

The magnificent estate home sat on several acres and was certainly big enough to handle such a large group of people. The grounds were impeccable. Since the weather was great, many guests mingled in the lavish gardens and around the Olympic-size pool, where fine linen-draped tables were decorated with lovely floral and candlelit centerpieces.

Dallas appeared in Lanier's vision, and he looked debonair in a black tuxedo. It didn't matter how many times she'd seen him in black-tie attire, she was still turned on by his gorgeous appearance. In fact, all the Carrington men looked hot in formal attire. Austin and Houston were off somewhere with Ashleigh and Kelly, and they had all arrived together in a white stretch limo. Beaumont and Angelica hadn't arrived yet.

Lanier's dark eyes stayed riveted on Dallas and the beautiful, curvaceous female who'd just come up to him. Throwing her milk-chocolate arms around his neck, she drew her leg up, resting her thigh against his. Lanier stiffened, disliking the provocative stance. She sat up ramrod-straight in the chair and settled into a position where she couldn't miss any action.

As the woman's ruby-red lips went to Dallas's ear, Lanier strained to hear what she said, although there was no chance of eavesdropping at such a distance. She could easily imagine that the woman was saying something sexy to her man.

Dallas looked totally uncomfortable as he did his best to extract himself from the willowy arms threatening to ruin one of the best nights of his life. He tried to turn back to get Lanier's attention, hoping she'd see how awkward this was for him, but the woman wasn't having it.

A couple of seconds later, the woman literally tried to pull Dallas out onto the ballroom dance floor. Digging in his heels, he strongly resisted her, but she was determined to have her way and kept pulling on him. Finally, he picked up the woman, set her aside, and then gave her a piece of his mind. Whatever he said to her earned him a dagger-sharp look. Just as Dallas turned and walked away, the woman shouted something at him that Lanier couldn't hear.

Dallas rapidly made his way over to Lanier, holding his hand out to her. "They're playing our song. The dance floor is calling us, sweetheart."

Lanier looked puzzled. "Since when did this become our song, Mr. Carrington?"

Dallas grinned. "Every love song is ours. I get excited every time I get an opportunity to bring you into my arms and hold you tight. Come dance with me."

Obeying his soft-spoken command, Lanier followed him and relaxed into his arms. She laid her head on his broad chest, loving how secure she felt. As he swept her over the dance floor, Dallas kept his arms wrapped around her.

As the slow song ended, loud shouting reached Lanier's ears. She turned around. Two sturdily built males swore loudly at each other, slurring their words.

Several men got between them and the arguing instantly stopped.

Horrible memories of the past came roaring back to Lanier as she looked on in horror, recalling the shouting and cursing of her own childhood. Barbara and Joseph used to verbally tear each other to shreds. She had been taught that once words left the mouth, they couldn't be recovered. Her mother had told her not to say or do anything she might have to apologize for later, yet Barbara had lived her life very differently. As her parents' arguments escalated, they'd go at each other physically.

Unable to bear her childhood memories, Lanier pulled away from Dallas and headed for an exit that led onto a marble terrace with a beautiful panoramic view. Until tears spilled onto the exposed flesh of her cleavage, Lanier hadn't realized she was crying. The disturbance inside had set her back many years. The volatile arguments that had occurred in her childhood home had suddenly resurfaced and began taking over her mind. She didn't want to relive those horrid times, especially when she desired to have the best future possible. Now it looked as if her dreams of a bright future had been threatened once again.

Would she ever be free from the shackles of her past?

Dallas came up behind Lanier and wrapped his arms around her waist. "It's okay, sweetheart. Everything's under control. Sorry you had to witness that madness."

At a loss for the right words, Lanier shivered. Fearing her voice would crack, she remained silent. The turmoil inside her stomach had her nauseated and terribly on edge.

How could she tune out the violence occurring inside her head?

"Why aren't you answering?" His nose nuzzled her neck. "What're you thinking, sweetheart? Wherever you are, please let me in."

Lanier tilted her head back against his chest. "I'm okay, Dallas. The ugliness just brought up bad memories."

Dallas wanted Lanier to understand that this episode wasn't the norm. If she was to end up his wife, she'd more than likely see some unpleasantness. "What you witnessed happens, Lanier, but it mostly occurs in the stands. People get too much to drink and then act out. Winning is not an excuse to get rowdy, but the participants in it look for any excuse to cause trouble. You've seen news stories about fans damaging public and private property after a major win. You've been to several formal events with me, and nothing like this occurred."

Lanier slowly turned around to face Dallas, resting her back against the cool iron railing. All she wanted was the comfort she found within the confines of his strong arms.

Dallas saw the depth of sadness in her eyes when she finally looked at him. "The violent behavior you saw is a downright disgrace to the owner and players. I don't even know who those men are, but the owner will find out."

As much as Lanier would like to know who the men were that started the altercation, she figured it didn't matter. She knew that neither man involved was a member of the Hurricanes.

Looking into his eyes, Lanier smoothed Dallas's hair

with the palm of her hand. "I know you can't control it, but it still unnerves me. I've lived in so many violent homes."

"I know you have, and I'm sorry you had to endure that way of life. But that's all over now. You don't ever have to be around those kinds of people. I'd never insist on you coming to a team function, knowing your fears. And I'd be happy to stay away, too. I only want to be with you, wherever you are."

Tears welled in Lanier's eyes. "You're so sincere. It's hard for me to be around rowdiness. I have a hard time with what went on inside because it brings back bad memories. I don't want to live like that."

Dallas felt a hidden meaning lurking within Lanier's remarks.

Would she dare give up a life with me because of bad behavior in my profession? It exists in all walks of life, not just in the lives of the rich and famous.

Dallas dropped several kisses atop Lanier's head. "We can go home if you don't feel comfortable staying. The dinner and awards ceremony is over and there are no more speeches tonight. I won't miss a thing if we leave."

Lanier tenderly kissed Dallas's mouth. "I wouldn't think of ending your well-deserved evening. If I felt that strongly about leaving, I'd call a cab." She kissed him again. "You earned this special celebration. As always, you were brilliant!"

Dallas bowed from the waist, tipping a nonexistent hat. "Thank you very much. This is our third pennant win, yet none of the others felt this good. Want to know why?"

"Why?"

"You're sharing it with me. Success is nothing more than a good feeling without someone special to celebrate with. Thanks for being here for me."

Dallas's comments had Lanier all choked up. Too emotional to relay her thoughts verbally, she kissed him passionately, showing him how happy she was to be there for him and with him. Dallas was the only man for her.

Lanier, Ashleigh, Kelly and Angelica escaped to one of the mansion's twelve luxurious bathrooms to freshen up their makeup. Inside a spacious sitting room, plush velvet benches in royal purple looked invitingly comfortable.

Kelly chuckled. "I wonder who the chick was that made a fool of herself earlier."

Wishing Kelly hadn't brought up the ugly incident, Lanier's smile rapidly turned into a rancid frown. She refreshed her lipstick but didn't comment.

Ashleigh gave Kelly a slightly scolding look, letting her know the remark was in poor taste. She did not want to see her friend's evening ruined by some mindless female who didn't seem to care how cheaply she portrayed herself in public.

As the four women left the bathroom, that very woman entered. Stopping abruptly, she stared Lanier up and down. "I agree with my girlfriends—Dallas can do much better for himself. You must be willing to do things in the bedroom most women wouldn't consider. What a waste of his precious time."

Lanier turned and glared at the woman.

Noticing Lanier's balled-up fists, Ashleigh intervened. "Let's not dignify rudeness. It's obvious she never learned how to carry herself with class." With that said, Ashleigh steered Lanier out the door.

"Thanks, Ashleigh," Lanier remarked. "I wouldn't have gone off on her, but I wanted to. I'd never embarrass myself, Dallas or any other Carrington like that."

Ashleigh took hold of Lanier's hand. "I know that. Speaking of our guys, I wonder where they are."

"Austin is coming this way right now," Kelly said. "He just spotted you."

Turning in the direction Kelly had pointed, Ashleigh's eyes lit up. "Look at him. Isn't he the most gorgeous man you've ever laid eyes on?"

"One of three," Angelica said. "My sons are amazing. Don't leave out Beaumont!"

Everyone laughed.

Austin came up to Ashleigh and kissed her. "I was looking for you. Where were you?"

"Restoring my pretty face," Ashleigh flirted. "These hot lights are melting the skin right off my face," she joked, batting her eyelashes. "I missed you."

"As much as I missed you?" Austin asked his wife.

Ashleigh ran her hand down the side of his face. "More. Where are your clones?"

Austin shrugged. "Don't know. I haven't seen them for a minute. They'll pop up. Is everyone having a good time?" His gaze encompassed all the ladies.

"It's been fun," Lanier enthused. "This house is to die for."

Ashleigh gave Lanier a sympathetic look. "We were

having a ball until we ran into a lady with a nasty mouth."

"Correction," Lanier said. "By no means was she was a lady."

Laughter broke out among the women. Then Ashleigh quickly explained to Austin what had occurred in the bathroom.

"Sorry to hear that. You beauties are envied by lots of women. I hope you didn't take the encounter to heart, Lanier. Dallas loves you, only you."

"Did I just hear my name?" Dallas walked up behind Lanier and wrapped his arms around her. Lowering his head, he kissed her neck and ears. "You disappeared. Where'd you go?"

Tilting her head back, Lanier looked up at Dallas. "Ladies' room, where we ran into an unladylike sister."

Dallas frowned. "Does anyone know her?"

"Hmm, you might. Since she had you all hemmed up earlier," Lanier remarked.

Dallas felt a stab of anger rush through him, yet he was impressed by Lanier's demeanor. She didn't seem upset by whatever had occurred. "Don't sweat it, babe. I don't even know her. This is the first time I've ever seen the woman…and I hope it's the last."

"Not if she has her way. She seems to think you can do much better than me."

Dallas heard a twinge of pain in Lanier's voice. "She's wrong. You're the best for me…and I'm the best for you."

Lanier kissed Dallas full on the mouth. "That you are. You're a blessing to me."

"You feel that way, too, huh?" Dallas kissed her back.

He then rubbed his stomach. "I'm starving. Let's go find something to eat."

Lanier smiled softly. "You go ahead and grab a bite. I'll be right here."

Dallas lifted an eyebrow. "You're not hungry?"

Lanier shook her head. "Not now. I may get something later on."

Dallas kissed the tip of Lanier's nose. "Don't stray too far. I won't be gone long."

She pointed out a couple of empty seats. "I'll post up right here and wait for you."

He kissed her gently on the mouth and then strode off.

Lanier sat down on one chair and placed her bag on the other to reserve it. As her mind took her back to the bathroom scene, she cringed. Lanier knew she shouldn't give any thought to the injurious remarks, but it was difficult to ignore the intent behind them, especially when it had hurt her.

Perhaps Dallas *could* do better. But if that woman thought she was better, she would've been in for a rude awakening. Any woman who didn't care about people wouldn't attract Dallas. He wanted a woman like his mother. Lanier knew she wasn't just like Angelica, but the other female wasn't close to being the woman Mrs. Carrington was. Not only was she a wonderful wife and fantastic mother, but she was a pillar in her community.

Hearing loud talking, Lanier looked to the left of her and saw one of the men from earlier. She was surprised he hadn't been ushered out and told to leave the premises, since he clearly was a disruptive force. He was staggering quite a bit. It was hard to understand much of anything he said because he was mumbling. His stumbling around drew the attention of others.

The tall man suddenly staggered forward and fell down close to Lanier's feet. What looked like a full glass of red wine splashed onto her white dress and the stain spread rapidly, covering a large area. He looked up at her and said something she didn't understand. The next thing she heard was him calling her a dirty name. Picking up her purse, she attempted to stand.

As he tried to get up, too, he fell into Lanier again and knocked her over. Several men rushed to her side to help her up. Fear ripped through her and she suddenly felt frozen in time. She didn't need to close her eyes to experience the violent visions and malicious verbal attacks that had kept her upset.

The man had sounded just like Joseph when he had slurred his words. She was no stranger to the stumbling and staggering she'd witnessed repeatedly. Going into a darkened closet to hide and shut out the vulgar shouting was all too familiar. The thought of fleeing into a hiding place had already entered her mind. Though scared of the darkness, it had been more comforting to her than what she had witnessed from her parents.

No young child should ever be faced with the choice of escaping into darkness versus seeing and hearing violence. Both options were frightening to her, but the darkness was the lesser of two evils for her. Inside the closet was a pillow she'd laid her head upon while she was curled up in a fetal position. Lanier hadn't always been successful at blocking out the sounds of violence and vicious yelling and disrespectful name-calling.

Hoping to flee from the disturbing images, Lanier

tried to take flight toward the nearest exit. Her legs felt locked in place and vehement memories surrounded her. Finally, her feet managed to break into a full run…and she didn't stop moving forward until she got outside, where she then took a minute to catch her breath.

Somewhat dazed, she descended the steps and walked toward the parking area. Once she located the Carrington limo and its driver, she began to breathe easier.

With her hands shaking badly, Lanier approached the driver. "Please, can you take me home and then come back for the others? I'm not feeling well. Mr. Carrington knows I'm leaving," she lied, feeling terrible about it. Getting as far away from this mansion and the drunk inside was all she could think about. She'd felt threatened too many times in one evening. Re-experiencing the horrible memories of the darkest time of her life was extremely unpleasant.

"Of course, ma'am, I'll take you home. I'll let one of the Carrington brothers know I'm leaving the area. That's what they'd expect from me."

"Dallas already knows. Can we please leave now? I'm only getting worse. Mr. Carrington knows how bad I'm feeling."

The chauffer looked torn by what he believed was the right thing to do versus what was required of him. He had been hired by the triplets and thought he should take orders only from them. He felt that the stain on her white dress was in part responsible for her stressful demeanor. "It won't take me long to locate one of them." Without further comment, the chauffer went off to find one of the brothers.

Totally stressed by the situation, Lanier suddenly swooned. She quickly grabbed on to the car's door handle to keep from falling. Able to keep her footing, she checked the rear entry to see if it was open. Finding the limo unlocked, she got in immediately.

Lanier laid her head back against the headrest. She kept going over what had happened inside, which made it hard for her to let go of it. Knowing what Dallas may've done to the man after he'd knocked her over made her grateful he hadn't been a witness.

She tried to remind herself that the man didn't know her. He had reacted to the alcohol, a lot like Barbara and Joseph had done. Her mother had been a peaceful person before she'd begun drinking and drugging. It had been shocking to see her turn violent and nasty. Many of the obscenities spewed out of her mother's mouth had put Lanier in a state of disbelief. The names Barbara had called Joseph were every bit as bad as the ones she herself had been called this evening. Two people had lived inside her parents' bodies, two totally different individuals. She wondered if the strangers that had taken over her mother and father were truly gone.

Were Barbara and Joseph really back to their old, kind, loving selves?

Dallas slid into the backseat and sat close to Lanier. Concern was etched on his face. As he tried to put his arm around her, he felt her resistance. "What happened in there to make you run away without telling one of us?" Noticing the large red stain on her dress gave him a good idea why she'd left the party. Now he needed to know how the dress had been ruined.

His tone had sounded accusatory to Lanier. She pointed at the stain. "It should be obvious. While you were off doing who knows what, I was dealing with one of the drunken men from earlier. That's who spilled the wine on my dress. Do you need to interrogate me further?"

"Interrogate? Is that what you think I'm doing? Dumb question, since it's obvious. Asking you why you left is only one question. An interrogation is a barrage of inquiries."

Old childhood memories had helped Lanier's negativity to resurface. She couldn't help wondering if he was embarrassed by her actions. Because he'd left her alone on several occasions she had begun asking herself where he had gone and what he had been doing.

Was it possible he actually knew the woman who'd made the nasty remarks? If she didn't know him, how would she know he could do better? Better than what?

Negative thinking had finally led Lanier back to Casey's comments, making her wonder which one of them hadn't been telling the truth.

"Maybe you're the one who should be interrogated. Why don't you tell me why you disappeared so much in there? You left me alone a lot, which put me at the mercy of others."

Dallas couldn't believe her questions—and her negative misgivings had him fuming inwardly. "I left your side three times. Getting drinks for us was one. Using the men's room was another. Lastly, I went to find more food. I couldn't have been gone more than ten to fifteen minutes each time. What happened to the new Lanier?

Speaking of interrogations, is there anything else you want to question me about?"

Lanier's eyes burned with fury. "As a matter of fact, I have several questions. Do you know the woman who was all over you? And have you been flirting with Casey and trading flirtatious emails with her like she says? I also find it odd that a woman you don't know would say you can do better than me if she doesn't know you."

Dallas glared back at her. "This one takes the cake. I've had it with all this negative energy. I can't do this anymore. You are never going to fully trust me. No matter what I do to show you I love you, no matter how many times I tell you, you still don't believe me."

Dallas slid across the seat and exited from the door he'd entered. He stopped for a minute, trying to get his anger in check. His heart wanted him to take her in his arms and disprove what it knew she believed. But as he pondered the things she'd asked him, he got even angrier. At this point, taking her into his arms was the worst idea, especially since she'd resisted his touch earlier. Trying to help Lanier get rid of her negative thinking was absolutely futile. Although it was something he had never wanted to believe, she hadn't left him with any reason to be hopeful. He hadn't been able to change her mind. Beating a dead horse was useless. It was time for him to let go—and bitterness and frustration had him slamming shut the car door.

Dallas walked over to the limo driver. "Please take Miss Watson home. Her dress is ruined and she's really upset. The rest of us are staying until midnight, when the party ends."

Understanding the situation, the driver nodded. "I'll take her home and return."

Later that night, Dallas wore a brooding expression, as he sat up front with the driver. His brothers were in the back with Ashleigh and Kelly. He'd sat up front to keep from ruining their good moods. He was less upset that the woman he loved had tried to leave the party without telling him. Being taken down to the mat about Casey and another woman that he didn't even know had hurt him deep inside. She hadn't once mentioned that leaving her alone made her uncomfortable. Lanier made it seem like she was accusing him of hooking up with the woman who had insulted her.

Lanier's mistrust of him had always been painful to deal with, but he'd begun to feel better when it looked as if he was making some progress. If it wasn't clear to him before, he was dead wrong, and that was now crystal clear. He'd put so much energy into getting her to trust him, but he'd failed miserably. He couldn't win this battle and he didn't see this war continuing. He wasn't embarrassed by Lanier, had never been ashamed of her, yet she believed he was. All she would've had to do was tell him she wanted to leave. Earlier in the evening he had assured her of that very thing.

Why hadn't she trusted me enough to tell me what had occurred? Trust was the issue.

She had actually blamed him for leaving her alone to fend for herself. He hadn't been gone for more than a few minutes each time.

Lanier just wasn't getting it, nor was she feeling him. Dallas was starting to realize he wasn't the one to help her get it. He couldn't make her confident, nor could he get her to move out of the shadows of her past and into the future. He wasn't embarrassed by her leaving; it was just how she'd gone about it.

Lanier was too beautiful of a woman to walk among dark shadows and ashes.

Dallas bid farewell to Ashleigh, Kelly and his brothers at his house. Before he reached the front door, he heard Austin calling out to him. He walked a few steps back to meet his brother.

Austin put his hand on Dallas's shoulder. "Man, we know some of what happened tonight, but we don't understand why you won't tell us everything. We're your brothers, and there isn't anything you can't share with us."

Dallas sighed. "It's a private matter, Austin. Let it go."

Austin feigned a punch at Dallas. "Like hell I will. You're obviously upset. Houston and I aren't leaving here until we know what happened to send Lanier running from the party. I know there was a woman who'd said some pretty nasty things to her, but that happened early on—and she'd seemed fine afterward."

Dallas had a pleading look on his face. "Don't leave your wife waiting like this, Austin. I'm sure Ashleigh is worried enough about Lanier. Don't give her anything more to fret about."

"Okay, I won't. Go on in the house, but you need to answer the doorbell when I ring it. If you don't, I *will* use my emergency key. Take it as a threat or a promise. It'll be fulfilled."

Determined to get to the bottom of his brother's problems, Austin walked back to the limo and got inside. The anxious look on his wife's face broke his heart. "It'll be okay, sweetheart. Dallas needs us tonight. Houston, we need to stay with our brother. We've never left each other alone during dark times. The driver can take Ash and Kelly home. We can drive one of Dallas's cars back to the ranch."

"Houston, I'll go to the ranch with Ashleigh and wait for you, if that's okay," Kelly said.

"I'd love that," Ashleigh remarked before Houston responded.

Smiling, Kelly nodded. "I'll stay until the guys get back."

"It may take us a while, Kelly," Houston remarked. "We're not leaving here until Dallas is in much better shape."

Ashleigh laid her hand on top of Houston's. "Kelly can spend the night in a guest cabin or in a guest room inside the main house. We'll figure it out. Now go and help Dallas. He needs you guys, whether he's admitting it or not."

Austin and Houston kissed the women before exiting the limo. They exchanged worried glances as they approached Dallas's front door.

Dallas hated that he had inconvenienced his brothers, but he was happy to have the support. Seated on the leather sofa in his family room, he explained what he'd heard about Lanier's experience with the intoxicated man. "He's the same guy that was involved in the earlier brawl. I don't know who he is, and neither do my teammates. Did you guys know him?"

Both Austin and Houston shook their heads.

"What are you the most upset about, Dallas?" Austin asked.

"The mistrust in me that Lanier continues to harbor. It's so unfounded and totally baseless. I've never done anything to make her distrust me. I'm tempted to go over to Haven House and have it out with her, but it'll end badly if I go now. I'm too upset to be rational. Besides, it's after two in the morning. If she wanted to talk, she could've reached me on my cell."

Houston pressed his lips together. "What else do you want from her, Dallas? You already know what she's been through. She can't seem to shake her horrible past…and that's understandable. You may have to be patient for years to come."

Dallas's features took on the appearance of a dark thundercloud. "I don't have to do that…and I won't. It's past time for Lanier to grow up. She can't continue using what happened eons ago as an excuse to keep me waiting and wondering. I want a wife and kids. She can't handle that right now. I don't know why I fell for the so-called changes. She either can't change her circumstances, or she refuses to."

Houston looked worried. "What are you really saying, man? Do you hear yourself?"

"It's the end of the road for me. I'm out. I'm not getting any younger. I want a wife, one who'll love and cherish me as much as I will her. I don't want to be a crutch for Lanier or any other woman. I've given enough of myself. I've been committed. It's obvious to me that she isn't. Lanier Watson is living in the past. I live in the moment, and I want to look ahead to a future. It's really that simple."

Austin raised both eyebrows. "Are you saying it's over between you two?"

Tears sprang to Dallas's eyes. "The message I'm getting is that I don't matter. It's all about her and what she needs and wants. What about me? Lanier is clearly not thinking of my feelings. Words of love are easy for her to say, but she can't act on them. I'm done."

"Dallas," Houston shouted, "how can you say you love Lanier and give up on her so easily? Time and time again you've told us that you're in it for the long haul. Were you lying?"

Dallas was stunned by Houston's angry outburst. Austin wasn't shouting, but he was obviously upset.

"I was lying to myself. I love her and want her more than anyone can know. What I don't need is the baggage weighing us down. It's too heavy a load to carry. I've been toting it around for a long time now. Lanier is not even trying to lighten our load."

Austin's eyes narrowed. "How can you say that?"

Dallas slapped his hand down hard on his thigh. "There must be some sort of payoff for her to keep this baggage around. Is Lanier lying about how she feels about me? I'm starting to believe she is. Maybe she simply doesn't know how to feel. Is she so numb by past hurts that she'll never feel again? I'm not willing to deal with an emotionless relationship, not where I'm the only one who feels anything."

Austin stood. "Sounds like you've made up your mind. If Lanier can't give you what you need, I understand why you'd walk. If you need me, just pick up the phone or drop by."

"I second that," Houston said. "I'm here for you, Dallas. We're only a phone call and a few miles away. Want us to spend the night? I know Kelly and Ash will understand our need to be here. We'll make that call if you want."

Dallas shook his head. "Thanks, guys. I love you. I can deal with the fears of my decisions about Lanier. I'll worry about her. I may love her for the rest of my life, but I won't accept less for me than what I give out."

"I hate to see it end this way," Austin said. "Good night, Dallas."

As soon as Austin and Houston walked out, Dallas closed the door. Seconds later, he broke down. Never before in his entire life had he cried that hard or felt that much agony.

Chapter 12

Dallas took a couple of days to reckon with his decision before he stopped by for a visit with Lanier. As they sat in her family room, the tension between them was thick and oppressive. No warm hugs had been exchanged at the door. Smiles were now strained. He'd arrived several minutes ago, but not a word since *hello* had passed their lips.

Knowing it was time to get it over with, Dallas cleared his throat. "I'm sorry it had to come to this, but, Lanier, I can't stay in this relationship. We're obviously not meant for each other. We've made no progress in deciding on our future as a couple. That's a huge problem for me. I'm tired of waiting on something I may never have."

Lanier picked at nonexistent lint on her slacks. "I understand, Dallas," she finally said, getting to her feet.

"I can't blame you. You deserve someone who can love you unconditionally."

Dallas wished Lanier had said something profound. If she'd fought for him, he would've given in so easily. His life was miserable without her. He stood. "You're a beautiful woman, and you're smart and talented. I see it, but you don't. The reason you can't recognize it is beyond me. I've waited on you a long time. I'm so unhappy that it's all been in vain."

"I know you've waited. I appreciate it." Lanier fought the tears. "I'll be okay. I've been like this all along… and I've survived. I don't expect anything good to come into my life."

"That's so sad. I want to be with a happy Lanier, one who can put the past behind her and look forward to tomorrow. You deserve to find love and happiness. You aren't happy and you can't give up the pain because you're addicted to it. Pain is your shield. That makes it impossible for me to get inside your heart. I tried to give you all the love I thought you'd ever need, yet I can't make you love yourself or me."

Walking over to Lanier, Dallas brought her into his arms and held her tight. He had rehearsed over and over again what he'd say to her, but none of what he'd practiced had come out. His heart had spoken for him, telling the truth as it was.

Lanier looked directly into Dallas's eyes. "Congratulations again on such a remarkable pennant win. I know how well the team is wearing the crown. MVP is a magnificent accomplishment for you. You earned it."

"Thanks for the compliments. I'll remember them always. I wish it could've been different for us. You and me together forever. I'm sorry it won't be. Good-bye, Lanier."

Standing on tiptoes, Lanier kissed Dallas's smooth, toffee-brown cheek, wishing she had the nerve to kiss his mouth. She loved him, but not enough to give up what helped to keep her strong. It was horrific, yet a foregone conclusion. By holding on to the pain, she'd never allowed herself to get hurt by anyone. The agony was a constant reminder of what to never let anyone do to her. This way, she was safe.

It's you, Dallas. It'll always be you. No one will ever have my heart. It belongs to you.

Out in the foyer, Lanier and Dallas kissed, but the passion was missing. As she closed the door behind him, tears slid from her eyes. Crying hard, she made her way back into the family room and took the seat Dallas had occupied.

Dallas's remarks hurt Lanier deeply, yet she hadn't been surprised. She'd gotten the message after he'd failed to call her or come by long after the party was over. She felt all alone, and she only had herself to blame.

The girls had recently called home to say they were going to a college roommate's home for Thanksgiving weekend. They also planned to go to Europe for Christmas with a group of young women they'd become close friends with. The large sum of money given to them by the Carrington family would certainly come in handy on a European holiday.

Being alone for both holidays would be a major drag for Lanier, but she'd never hold the girls back. For their kids to live the best life possible and have wonderful experiences was what their foster care program was about. Life was lonelier, and she was hurting something terrible, but she'd made a career out of living with both.

It was now early November. The city of Houston's temperatures were much cooler but perfect for early-morning or evening walks. Lanier, Ashleigh and Kelly had just finished having dinner in Ashleigh's formal dining room. The threesome had gotten together to catch up. Austin had prepared a tenderloin roast and baked potatoes for the women to enjoy.

The triplets had gone to a special tribute for a Baseball Hall of Famer, and they weren't expected back before midnight. Baby Austin was with his grandparents for the night. Lanier wouldn't have accepted the invite to dinner if there'd been a chance of running into Dallas. Her friends hadn't talked a lot about what had gone down between Lanier and Dallas because Lanier wasn't open to it. Everything was still too raw for her.

Ashleigh stood. "Let's relax in the family room. Does anyone want coffee?"

"Coffee for me," Lanier said.

"Me, too," Kelly chimed in.

Ashleigh decided to clear the table later. She wanted to spend quality time with her friends. She'd seen Kelly a lot, but Lanier had become somewhat of a recluse, and she only saw her on visits to Haven House. Social events had been scrapped from Lanier's calendar, which Ashleigh hated. Lanier had been a huge part of her life. The distance was hard on both friends.

Lanier walked over to Ashleigh and put an arm

around her shoulder. "Let me get the coffee for you. You've done enough hosting for one evening."

Ashleigh knew not to protest. No one wanted her doing anything while she was pregnant, and they all hovered over her like they were fearful she'd break in two. Kelly was as bad as the rest of the family. Ashleigh didn't like all the needless attention, but she knew any objections would fall on deaf ears.

Ashleigh didn't bother to move a muscle as her friends came back into the family room. By the length of time passed, she figured they'd also cleaned up the kitchen. Having poured chilled orange juice for the young mommy, Lanier handed it to Ashleigh.

Ashleigh smiled at Lanier. "You're still on top of my needs. Thank you."

Lanier smiled back. "I want you healthy."

Ashleigh knew her friend loved her despite her inability to share her love with others who desperately needed her, namely Dallas. Lanier loved Dallas more than anything in the world, yet her past had held her back from giving him her all. Dallas hadn't dated anyone since Lanier, and no one had dared to try to set him up with anyone.

Wondering if she should ask the burning question on her mind, Lanier bit down on her lower lip. *Bite the bullet,* she told herself. "How is Dallas?"

Ashleigh shrugged. "He's fine. Our boy still hasn't come down from the upcoming trip to the World Series, but that's to be expected." She grew quiet for a moment. "How are you? That is, without Dallas around?"

Taking a few seconds to form an honest answer, Lanier sighed. "Opened up Pandora's box, didn't I? I'm fine, too, but only when I'm busy. The minute there's a lull in my day or evening, I cry my heart out. I miss him. He's in my heart to stay."

Ashleigh and Kelly found it hard not to cry over Lanier's broken heart. Lanier already regretted the question she'd asked Ashleigh. She and Dallas were over. Never again would they discuss wedding plans, though she still wanted to marry him and live happily ever after. She knew that she'd ruined things for them, and the thought always made her cry.

Ashleigh saw the tears. "Sorry I upset you." Ashleigh went over and took Lanier's hand, escorting her to the sofa, where they both sat down. "You began the conversation, so I thought it was okay to discuss it. I know you're not okay. You don't have to pretend with us."

Kelly still had hopes that the couple could end up together. She took Lanier's other hand. "Close your eyes and imagine this. Three gorgeous men standing at the altar, waiting on the women they love to come down the church aisle. Conjure up an amazing image of you, Ashleigh and me floating down a rose-petal-strewn aisle to meet up with the wonderful men of our dreams, the men we love as much as life itself. Keep your eyes closed until you can clearly envision a wedding."

"Imagine it just the way you'd love your wedding day to be, Lanier," Ashleigh added. "Think about me, your best friend, standing with you at the altar, holding your hand. Think of Kelly standing with us, as we all let tears of joy flow free. Focus your mind on Dallas's unconditional love for you. On that special day he will take you as his wife and you'll take him as your husband."

Tears trickled down Lanier's face. As hard as she tried to see what Ashleigh and Kelly told her to imagine, she couldn't. Dallas turned into Joseph and she had changed into Barbara, a hateful scowl on her face. "All I see is us turning into my parents," Lanier said, lost in a haze of confusion.

Pressing Lanier's head against her and trying to keep from crying, Ashleigh held on tightly to her dearest friend. "I'm sorry things went badly, Lanier. You and Dallas are a match made in heaven. We all know it. And you *will* see it for yourself one day. I know you will. You are not Barbara, and Dallas is not Joseph."

Kelly felt awful since she was the one who'd started pressing Lanier's imagination into service. It had been a disastrous idea, even if she did think Lanier and Dallas were an amazing couple. Until Lanier recognized their relationship for what it was, no one could make her see the beauty of it.

Lanier got up from the sofa. "Excuse me for a minute, you two. I'll be back. And I *will* be okay." Lanier blew kisses to Ashleigh and Kelly.

"I know you will," Ashleigh said. "I know it in my heart."

Inside the hall bathroom, Lanier stared unflinchingly into the mirror. Engaged in a war with her own image, she continued to stare at it without batting a lash. "You *are* beautiful. Your spirit and your mind *are* beautiful. Dallas is everything any man could ever dream of being. He has more compassion in his little finger than some folks have in their entire bodies. You *will not* compare him to Joseph, and there are *no* comparisons between Barbara and you."

Lanier put her head down. Then, lifting her head high, she stared into the mirror again. "I take that back. There are no comparisons between you and the sick woman who long ago traded places with Barbara. The real Barbara has come back to claim her life and her daughter. Me, Lanier Watson, the daughter of Joseph and Barbara Watson, can finally step into the future."

Lanier wet a paper towel and wiped her face off. She couldn't repair her makeup since she hadn't brought her purse into the bathroom. "That's okay. You look beautiful without any makeup, Lanier Watson. According to Dallas Carrington, you have natural beauty, inside and out. And Dallas loves every part of you."

Practically running back into the family room, Lanier's smile glowed like sunshine. "Are you guys ready to get back to planning our triple wedding? Dallas said it was over, and he's never going to ask me to marry him again. But I thought about it, and I can't let him go like this. I'm going to ask him to marry me. Can you two go shopping with me tomorrow to help pick out his ring?"

Ashleigh and Kelly jumped up from the sofa.

"I'm in," Kelly said with enthusiasm.

Ashleigh had tears in her eyes as she hugged Lanier. "You already know my answer, Lanier. It's a resounding yes!"

Nearly two weeks after her dinner with Ashleigh and Kelly, Lanier stood at Dallas's front door. She had just said a prayer, asking for help through the most important moment of her life. Smoothing her chic black pantsuit, she waited on Dallas to open the door.

The door opened slowly. "How can I help you?" asked the female with a sultry voice.

Lanier stared at the beautiful woman standing before her. Her first thought was to run. Then she squared her shoulders and made direct eye contact with the woman. "Is Dallas in?"

The woman looked a bit surprised. From the visitor's initial reaction, she had expected her to bolt. "Can I tell him who's here to see him?"

The woman who loves him, the same woman he loves back. That's who wants to see him.

Lanier smiled. "Tell him it's Lanier Watson. He'll know the name."

"Okay. Why don't you step into the foyer while I find him? I'll be right back."

The thought of running came to Lanier's mind again. Once more, she stood her ground.

It is now or never. Today is a gift, and tomorrow isn't promised.

Lanier could hear the woman calling Dallas's name. Her palms were sweaty now, but her resolve was steely. She lifted her head high and squared her shoulders, something she'd gotten into the habit of doing when negativity tried to invade her soul.

Dallas stopped dead in his tracks when he saw Lanier in the foyer. *Oh, my God! She's more beautiful than ever. Look at her!* He'd never had to ask himself why he loved her because he'd always known. Lanier was the woman meant for him. She was standing inside his home and that meant something. It was now time to find out exactly what that something was.

Dallas moved toward her, his hands outstretched. Taking both of her hands in his, he kissed each of her cheeks. "You're still so beautiful! How are you?" He paused a moment. "Please come on in and have a seat. I'd love to know what's been happening in your life since we last saw each other."

Relief flooded through Lanier at the warm reception, making her weak in the knees. Standing on tiptoes, she kissed Dallas lightly on the mouth. "Thank you. I'm glad you're willing to see me."

"I can't think of a single reason why I'd turn you away." Dallas smiled, directing her toward the formal living room. "You're here, so let's catch up."

Acting as the gentleman he was, Dallas waited until Lanier was seated before he sat down next to her on the sofa. The scent of her perfume drove him wild, and his libido reacted instantly. "How are you, Lanier?"

Daring to look him in the eyes, Lanier pushed nervous hands down her thighs. "I'm fine. In fact, I've never been better. Life is good."

Loving the confident way she spoke, he sighed with relief. "Glad to hear it. Tell me what you've been up to. I want to know everything."

Lanier put a finger to her right temple. "Let me see. Where should I start? I got it," she said with enthusiasm. "First off, I'm thinking of building a house on the property surrounding Haven House. I've been talking with an architect about drawing up plans."

"How's it been for you without the girls?"

Lanier hunched her shoulders, swallowing hard. "It's

hard. I enjoyed having them under my care, and I really love them. It was a very demanding undertaking at first, but I'm ready to do it again. As you know, Ashleigh and I put Haven House on the emergency list."

"Sounds like you're doing great. Do you have any other important news?"

Lanier nodded. "It's actually good news. I've been seeing a new therapist. He's good with me and has helped me a lot. Reality checks are much easier for me now." As she thought about her problems with Casey, she decided not to tell Dallas how she'd gone there and had given her hell over the games she'd been playing with them. *That was in the past.*

Dallas stroked his chin. "What made you change therapists?"

"My old one wasn't a good fit for me. She shared with me a few of her own emotional problems, and some of hers were bigger and more intense than mine. Several of our issues were similar."

Lanier's eyes connected with his. She quickly looked away to break the spell she was already succumbing to. "What about you? What's been happening in your life?"

And who is the eye candy that opened the door? Better yet, who and what is she to you?

"I'm not through finding out what's going on with you yet. We'll get to me. Where do things stand with you and your parents?"

Lanier smiled. "Things are good. I've gotten close to my mother and I've forgiven my dad, though I never thought I could."

"That's great news, Lanier. Forgiveness is an important part of living."

"I know. I learned that the hard way. My mother was infected with Joseph's diseases, alcoholism and addiction, but they're both working seriously at a twelve-step program. I go to a meeting with them once a month, and I've also joined a support group for family members. In short, we're all getting the help we need."

"Wow! That is fantastic news. How are the girls doing in school, and are they still coming home for the holidays?"

Lanier filled Dallas in on the latest with the girls, who still loved her enough to keep her in the loop. "They going to Europe for Christmas, and I've been abandoned for Thanksgiving. I've had a couple of invitations to Thanksgiving dinner, but I think I'll just have a quiet day at home. It seems easier that way. Maybe I'll invite my parents to dinner."

"You and your parents should join our family. Mom and Dad would love to have all of you. So would I. Will you at least think about it?"

"I will," she said, without the slightest hesitation. "Where is dinner being held?"

"Right here. All three of us are hosting it together. We'll have Christmas at Austin's ranch. Ashleigh wants A.C. to have Christmas at home until he's older."

Lanier smiled. "That's our Ashleigh. She loves being a wife and a mom."

"You can say that again. They're such a happy family, and I don't expect it to ever change."

"Me, neither, Dallas. Those two are made for each other. Ashleigh tells me she and Austin want four kids. She wants to have them close together so they can grow up and have each other's backs."

"She has it all figured out. Austin loves kids. We try not to spoil A.C. rotten, but it's hard."

Lanier smiled gently. "I know what you mean. It was hard for me to keep from spoiling the girls. I'd even considered adopting them at one time, but they should have two parents."

"I agree." Dallas slapped his hand down on his thigh. "Please forgive my rudeness. Can I get you something to eat or drink?"

"Thank you, but I'm just fine. I should probably let you get back to your company."

"My company? Oh, you mean Althea. She's a cousin on our father's side, and she's visiting from Los Angeles for a couple of weeks. She's staying at our parents' home. Althea wants to be a movie star."

A whoosh of relief hit Lanier. Although she had tried not to dwell on the identity of the woman who'd opened the door, she was glad to know how she fit in with Dallas.

Dallas grinned broadly. "I'm glad you came here today. Was there another reason you came other than to stop by and say hello?"

Lanier licked her lips and her insides fluttered. "There's a very specific reason why I came. The most important one is to let you know how much I love you and that I've never stopped loving you. I'm not going to apologize for anything that happened because it was all a part of my growth. I love you, Dallas Carrington, wholeheartedly. I'm here to ask you to marry me."

Dallas was totally blown away. A myriad of questions rushed through his mind, but he didn't dare ask one of them, not when the woman he'd never stopped loving was waiting for an answer to her proposal.

Dallas smiled brightly. "No ring to offer?"

Wondering if he'd somehow heard that she'd been shopping for one, Lanier laughed. "As a matter of fact, there is a ring." Her hand wrapped around the velvet box in her purse and she brought it forth. Flipping it open, she showed the ring to Dallas. "Will you marry me, Dallas Carrington? Will you make me the happiest woman in the world by accepting this ring?"

Dallas dropped down in front of her on one knee. "Lanier Watson, I *will* marry you. Today, tomorrow, whenever you choose a date, I'll become your husband. I love you deeply."

Lanier's tears fell. "How does Christmas Eve sound?"

They both knew it was the day for Houston and Kelly's wedding and for Ashleigh and Austin to renew their vows. Dallas pulled Lanier forward and reclaimed the lips he'd longed to taste. "You have just made me the happiest guy alive. I can't believe this is happening."

"Believe it. On Christmas Eve, all the Carrington men will take vows, and I will become Mrs. Dallas Carrington!"

* * * * *

REQUEST YOUR FREE BOOKS!

2 FREE NOVELS
PLUS 2 FREE GIFTS!

KIMANI™
ROMANCE

Love's ultimate destination!

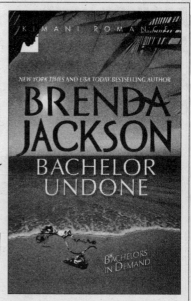

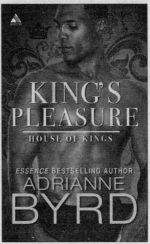

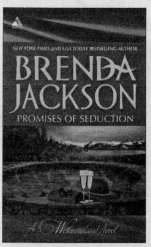